THE SON
THAT CHANGED
HIS LIFE

BY
JENNIFER TAYLOR

MILLS &
BOON

First published in Great Britain 2013
by Mills & Boon, an imprint of Harlequin (UK) Limited.
Harlequin (UK) Limited, Eton House,
18-24 Paradise Road, Richmond, Surrey TW9 1SR

© Jennifer Taylor 2013

ISBN: 978 0 263 89878 1

Harlequin (UK) policy is to use papers that are natural, renewable
and recyclable products and made from wood grown in sustainable
forests. The logging and manufacturing process conform to the
legal environmental regulations of the country of origin.

Printed and bound in Spain
by Blackprint CPI, Barcelona

Emily urged the little boy to his feet, holding his hand as she led him across the room. Ben crouched down, guessing it would be less intimidating for Theo if they were on eye level.

'Hello, Theo. It's nice to meet you,' he said softly. He held out the package he'd brought. 'This is for you.'

Theo stared at the parcel for a moment, then slowly reached out and took it from him. Kneeling down, he stripped off the paper, exclaiming in delight when he saw the bright red car that Ben had bought for him. Within moments he had the box open and was busily running it across the floor.

Emily laughed. 'You couldn't have bought him anything better. He adores cars.'

'Good. I'll make a note of that,' Ben said lightly, trying not to let her see how moved he was by his first proper encounter with his son.

'I'll carry on getting the supper,' Emily told him gently, and he could tell that she understood how he felt. He sighed. Nobody had ever been able to read him as well as Emily could.

It was something Ben knew he needed to bear in mind. He couldn't afford to do anything that might upset her. He had to concentrate on being a good father to Theo because that was all Emily wanted him to be: her son's father, not her lover. Would he be able to handle the change in their relationship? he wondered. In the past three years he had convinced himself that he was over her, that any feelings he'd had for her were dead. It had been easier that way, less painful. However, as he watched her leave the room, he felt his heart lurch.

Dear Reader,

I realised when I was planning this series that I was going to give Ben and Emily a really hard time, but I was confident that they were strong enough to overcome even the biggest obstacle a couple can face.

Discovering that Ben had cancer when he was younger comes as a huge shock to Emily. For the past three years she has tried to come to terms with the way he treated her, and now she has to revise her opinion of him. She realises that she still loves him and is thrilled when Ben admits that he loves her too, but having cancer has made Ben afraid to make a commitment. Although he longs to be with Emily and their son, he refuses to take the risk of hurting them.

Helping Ben and Emily overcome their fears and find a happy ending was a joy. Although their lives have been affected by cancer, it isn't a dark or depressing story—far from it. Their love for one another shines through and you just know that no matter what the future holds, they will face it together. I just hope you enjoy reading their story as much as I enjoyed writing it.

Best wishes,

Jennifer

Jennifer Taylor lives in the north-west of England, in a small village surrounded by some really beautiful countryside. She has written for several different Mills & Boon® series in the past, but it wasn't until she read her first Medical Romance™ that she truly found her niche. She was so captivated by these heart-warming stories that she set out to write them herself! When she's not writing, or doing research for her latest book, Jennifer's hobbies include reading, gardening, travel, and chatting to friends both on and off-line. She is always delighted to hear from readers, so do visit her website at www.jennifer-taylor.com

**These books are also available in eBook format
from www.millsandboon.co.uk**

CHAPTER ONE

HE HAD driven all night, wanting to avoid the worst of the bank holiday traffic. Now as he pulled up at the side of the road to watch the sun rise over the headland, Benedict Legrange could feel his doubts surfacing again. What did he hope to achieve by coming here? He knew the truth better than anyone did, so why waste his time? He wasn't the child's father. He couldn't be. The drugs he'd been given may have saved his life but they had left him infertile. He could never father a child and he *hadn't* fathered Emily's child, despite her claims to the contrary. So why put himself through all the heartache of seeing her again?

Ben sighed as he rested his head against the seat and closed his eyes. It was one thing to know he was behaving foolishly but something entirely different to stop himself doing so. Ever since his good friend Tom Bradbury had mentioned Emily, he had felt all churned up inside. It was almost three years since they'd had that brief affair, yet the memory of what had happened was as sharp as ever. Emily had touched him in ways no woman had ever done, affected him more deeply than he had believed possible. That was why he'd been so angry when she had told him she was expecting his child. He had known it was a lie and it had hurt—a lot!—to realise that she would try to deceive him.

A ray of golden light touched his lids and Ben opened his eyes. He breathed in deeply as he watched the sun climb above the headland. Bride's Bay in the summer was a beautiful place to be and he was determined to enjoy his visit. He was looking forward to seeing Tom again and to meeting Hannah and her son, Charlie. He smiled. Hannah had to be really special if she'd managed to make commitment-phobic Tom turn into a family man! Obviously the love of the right woman could have far-reaching consequences.

His smile faded abruptly. That wasn't something he had ever experienced. Emily hadn't loved him as her subsequent actions had proved. He had been merely a convenience, the man she'd hoped to con into accepting responsibility for the child she was carrying. It might have worked too if the circumstances had been different. He wouldn't have questioned her claims that he was the father if he hadn't known it was impossible. What had the consultant told him after he'd had that fertility test following his treatment, that the odds on him fathering a child were several billion to one? It had been a bitter blow. He loved children and he would have loved a child of his own so very much…

He shut off the thought because it was pointless going down that route. Whoever the child's father was, it wasn't him!

* * *

'Theo, no! Put that down right now… Oh!'

Emily Jackson made a grab for the carton of orange juice but she was a shade too slow. It landed on the kitchen floor, sending a wave of juice flowing across the tiles. Theo looked up at her with solemn dark brown eyes.

'Fall, Mummy.'

'So I can see, you little rip.' Emily grabbed a wad of kitchen roll and wiped up the juice. 'I know you were trying to help, darling, but you must wait for Mummy to pour your juice next time. Okay?'

'Okay.'

Theo smiled beatifically at her as he started to eat his cereal, and Emily didn't have the heart to berate him any further. After all what was a drop of spilled juice in the great scheme of things, she thought as she tossed the sodden paper into the bin. So long as Theo was happy and healthy she wasn't going to make an issue of it.

She helped him finish his breakfast then took him upstairs to clean his teeth, ever conscious of the minutes ticking away. Mornings were always hectic and today she needed to be at the surgery early as she had two patients booked in for fasting cholesterol tests. As soon as Theo had finished, she hurried him out to the car, quickly strapping him into his seat before fetching his lunch bag from the kitchen. Fortunately the good weather had held and there was no need to worry about coats, which saved another precious few seconds. It was just gone seven-thirty when she backed off the path of the tiny cottage she rented on the outskirts of the town and she breathed a sigh of relief. She'd be well in time for her first appointment after she'd dropped Theo off at the nursery.

She headed into Bride's Bay, taking the road that skirted the headland as it was the quickest route. There were already a number of cars about, no doubt tourists intent on making the most of the bank holiday weekend. She slowed down to let a top-of-the-range four-by-four turn into a narrow track leading to the cove. From the look of its paintwork the vehicle had never been off-road before and she smiled to herself as she pictured the state of the track's rutted surface. It wouldn't look quite so pristine after it had driven down there!

Emily rounded the bend then had to slow once again when she encountered a car parked on the grass verge. There were a couple of vehicles coming the other way so she waited for them to pass. She pulled out to overtake, automatically glancing at the car as she drew alongside. The driver had the window down and she had a clear view of him, so clear that for a moment she couldn't believe what she was seeing. Just for a second her brain seized up, the thoughts all jammed up like logs in a river: Ben. Here. Sitting in that car.

Her foot pressed down way too hard on the accelerator and she roared past, and the sound of the engine broke the spell. Emily bit her lip to stem the cry that threatened to emerge. She didn't want to frighten Theo but she could feel it building inside her until it felt her head was ringing with it. What did Ben want? Why had he come here? Did it have anything to do with Theo and if it did, how did she feel about that?

She took a deep breath, forcing the panic to subside to a level she could deal with. She had no idea what the answers were to any of those questions but she intended to find out.

'Have you got a minute, Tom?'

Emily summoned a smile as she popped her head round the consulting room door, but the tension that had been building inside her all morning was making her feel sick. It had been too busy to find out what Ben was doing in Bride's Bay before now and the uncertainty had been very hard to deal with. She knew that she wouldn't rest until she'd found out some answers.

'Of course. I just need to type up these notes and I'll be right with you.'

Tom Bradbury gave her a quick smile before he returned his attention to the computer screen and Emily did her best to curb her impatience. She went over to the window, concentrating on the view across the bay in the hope that it would calm her, but it didn't work. What did Ben want? Why had he come to Bride's Bay when it was the last place she would have expected to see him? He had made his position perfectly clear when she'd been to Paris to see him, so clear that she'd been left under no illusion that he didn't want anything more to do with her. So why had he come here when he must have known their paths would cross?

'Right, all done.' Tom spun his chair round and

grinned at her. 'It's been mad this morning, hasn't it? I had hoped that folk would have better things to do than worry about their ailments with the bank holiday coming up, but no such luck.'

'It doesn't work that way,' Emily told him, knowing that she couldn't just leap in and start demanding answers. She had to lead up to the subject, make it appear that it was of little consequence otherwise Tom would suspect something was wrong. That was the last thing she wanted. She'd told no one who Theo's father was, neither her family nor her friends knew he was Ben's son. She wasn't sure why she had kept it a secret but she'd felt it was better if nobody knew the truth. And there was no reason why she should change her mind at this point…was there?

She took a quick breath as yet another question tagged itself onto all the others and hurried on. 'With us being closed this afternoon as well as Bank Holiday Monday, a lot of people will have decided to make an appointment just in case.'

'You mean in case their cold turns to flu or their tickly cough to pneumonia?' Tom laughed. 'I never thought of that. Obviously, I've got a lot to learn about being a GP.'

'You seem to be coping well enough,' Emily assured him and he grinned.

'Thank you. I shall take that as a compliment. Anyway, what was it you wanted to see me about?' He looked enquiringly at her and Emily's mouth went dry.

All of a sudden she couldn't remember a word of her carefully rehearsed speech.

'I…erm…um.'

'Tom, darling, have you finished yet?'

She looked round when her friend Hannah Morris, another GP at the practice, came into the room, feeling a pang of something very much like envy strike her when she saw Tom's face light up. There was no doubt at all how he felt about Hannah or she about him and Emily couldn't help envying their closeness. It must be wonderful to have someone you could share your innermost feelings with…the way she'd once thought she could share hers with Ben.

'Yep. I just need to take these notes through to the office and that's it.' Tom stood up. 'I'm glad that Simon decided to cancel evening surgery. It's such a glorious day that I have to confess I don't feel like working.'

'It's a good job we aren't working,' Hannah stated, smiling up at him. 'Ben just phoned. Apparently, he's already here.'

'But I thought he wasn't arriving until this evening!' Tom exclaimed, mercifully missing Emily's gasp. Any hopes she may have harboured about being mistaken had just been shot right out of the sky. It definitely had been Ben in that car and now she needed to find out what he wanted.

'Me too, but it seems he decided to get an early start and drove through the night.' Hannah shrugged. 'He sounded a bit uptight, to be honest. I think he needs this break more than he's letting on.'

Emily frowned as she listened to the conversation. So Ben had come to Bride's Bay for a holiday? Was it true or was it an excuse? She had no way of knowing and it was another uncertainty to add to the ever expanding list.

'I thought that when I spoke to him the other day. He seemed rather...well, on edge, is the best way to describe it.' Tom suddenly turned and Emily hurriedly smoothed her face into what she hoped was a suitably noncommittal expression.

'You remember Ben Legrange, don't you, Emily? He stayed with Simon and Ros a couple of years ago while he was recuperating from some bug he'd picked up while working for Médecins Sans Frontières. I'm sure you were here at the time.'

'Yes, I was.' Emily summoned a smile, praying that her friends couldn't hear the strain in her voice. 'It was a few months after I'd returned to Bride's Bay to take up this job, in fact.'

'Of course.' Tom smiled at her. 'Hannah and I have invited him to stay for the weekend. He's been in London sorting out some problems with the funding for the clinic he's set up and we thought it would be nice if he had a couple of days on the coast before he returns to Paris.'

'There's nothing like a bit of sea air to recharge the batteries,' Emily agreed as calmly as she could. So that was the explanation. Ben was here for a break; it had nothing to do with her and Theo. The thought should have reassured her but it didn't. It was painful to know that she and Theo didn't figure in his life.

'Very true. And I have a feeling that Ben needs his batteries recharging more than most.' Tom sighed. 'He's been working flat out since his father died, setting up the clinic. I think he sees it as his duty to carry out his father's wishes no matter what the cost to him personally.'

'Which is why this break is all the more important,' Hannah said soothingly. She placed her hand on his arm. 'We'll make sure Ben enjoys himself, darling. A few days R & R and he'll be right as rain.'

'Of course he will.' Tom dropped a kiss on her nose then turned to Emily. 'How do you fancy helping us make Ben's visit that bit more special? We're planning a barbecue tomorrow night if the weather holds, so how about you and Theo coming along? I'm sure Ben would love to see you again and meet Theo, of course.'

Emily shook her head, feeling sick at the thought of her turning up with Theo in tow. If Ben hadn't wanted to acknowledge his son in private then he certainly wouldn't wish to do so in front of his friends. 'I'm afraid I have something planned tomorrow. Sorry.'

'Shame. If I'm not mistaken you two got on really well, didn't you?' Tom glanced at Hannah. 'Now that I think about it, I remember Ros saying that Emily and Ben seemed to have a real connection.' He laughed. 'I rather think Ros hoped it would turn into something more!'

Emily dredged up a smile when Hannah laughed but

it was all she could do not to let her friends see how much it hurt to hear that. She, too, had thought she and Ben had connected on a deeper level but she'd been wrong. All of a sudden she couldn't take any more and swung round, wanting to get away before she said something stupid. Nobody must know about her affair with Ben. Nobody must know that he was Theo's father either. It would only complicate matters and, worse still, start people talking. The last thing she needed was Theo overhearing some chance remark and getting upset.

'Emily, hold on.'

She stopped reluctantly when Tom called her back. 'Yes?'

'What did you want me for? You never said.'

'Oh. Do you know I've completely forgotten.' She gave a short laugh, doing her best to pretend that everything was fine even though it was far from being that. 'It can't have been anything important, can it?'

'Well, if you do remember then give me a call.' Tom put his arm round Hannah's shoulders and ushered her towards the door. 'Now we had better go and make Ben welcome. I think an afternoon lazing in the garden is called for, don't you?'

'Sounds like heaven,' Hannah assured him. She paused to glance back and Emily could see the gleam in her eyes. 'If you do change your mind about tomorrow night then you'll be very welcome, Emily. I'm sure Ben would love to see you.'

'Er…thank you, but as I said I've made other plans.'

Emily managed to hold her smile until they disappeared. She sighed. Tom and Hannah meant well but they had no idea of the problems they were creating by trying to push her and Ben together. Ben wasn't interested in her; he never had been. She'd been merely a convenience, someone to sleep with and discard once she'd outlived her usefulness. Although neither of them had allowed for the fact that she might get pregnant, it hadn't made any difference to Ben's plans.

She took a deep breath and made herself face the truth as she had faced it many times in the past few years. Ben had never wanted her. And he didn't want their son either.

CHAPTER TWO

'I HOPE it's all right. I'm afraid the room is rather small but the bed should be comfortable enough.'

'It's lovely. Thank you.'

Ben dredged up a smile, doing his best to behave like the perfect guest as he looked around the tiny attic room, but it was an effort. Had Emily recognised him this morning? He thought she had but in that case why hadn't she stopped? Why had she driven past without making any attempt to acknowledge him? Did she hate him so much that she couldn't even bear to speak to him?

The thought was more upsetting than it should have been, bearing in mind the way she had tried to trick him. Ben thrust it to the back of his mind as he turned to his hosts. Tom and Hannah had welcomed him with open arms and he should be content with that instead of wasting his time thinking about Emily. 'I'm sure I shall be very comfortable. I just can't help feeling guilty about putting you to so much trouble, though.'

'It's no trouble,' Hannah assured him and laughed. 'To be honest you've done me a favour. I've been nagging Tom to clear out the attic for ages but he only got round to doing it when he knew you were coming to stay!'

Ben laughed. 'It's good to know that I'm useful for something.'

'Oh, you are!' Tom clapped him on the shoulder. 'If it weren't for your visit then I doubt if Simon would have agreed to cancel evening surgery. The surveyors are coming this afternoon to start on the plans for the new health centre and he insisted that we'd be able to work round them. It was only when we mentioned that you were coming to stay that he had second thoughts.' Tom grinned as he swung little Charlie into his arms. 'It's thanks to you that we have the rest of the day off, my friend, and we're truly grateful. Now we shall leave you to settle in. We'll be in the garden so come and find us when you're ready.'

Ben tossed his bag onto the bed after his friends left. Walking over to the window, he stared across the roof-tops towards the bay. There were a number of boats tied up in the harbour, mostly fishing vessels although there were several pleasure craft too. The scene was so famil-iar that for a moment he was transported back to when he had first visited Bride's Bay. He had been too ill at first to appreciate the beauty of the small Devonshire coastal town; however, as his health had improved, he'd found himself increasingly drawn to the area. There was a raw beauty about the ever-changing vista of sea and sky that had touched something inside him…just as Emily had touched him.

Ben's mouth compressed. Whatever he'd thought he and Emily had had was an illusion. She'd had her own reasons for being with him and they'd had nothing to do with love. His blood ran cold even now at the thought of how he might have been duped. If he hadn't known he was infertile, he would have accepted the child as his own, brought him up, loved and cared for him, and unwittingly perpetuated her lie. Maybe she'd been desperate; he didn't know. But he could never forgive her for what she had tried to do. After all, it wasn't only him who would have lived her lie but her son, too. The boy would have grown up believing that Ben was his real father and that seemed like the worst kind of deception, to deny the child his true heritage.

Anger roared through him and he turned away from the view with a muffled curse. Leaving his bag on the bed he made his way downstairs. He would unpack later but right now he needed a distraction, pleasant company to take his mind off less pleasant matters. He went out into the garden, pushing thoughts of Emily and her deceitfulness from his mind. He wasn't going to waste the weekend by going over old ground. Maybe he had been a fool to come here but he wouldn't allow what had happened to rule his life. Tom was his closest friend and he didn't intend to let their friendship lapse. Maybe Emily did hate him, but so what? He couldn't have accepted the child as his own when he knew the truth.

Emily tiptoed out of the bedroom. It was just gone seven p.m. and for once Theo had fallen asleep without the usual tussle. Normally it took a while to settle him but he'd been worn out after an afternoon playing on the beach. Now the evening stretched before her and she sighed. It was this time when she felt most alone. It was fine during the day; she was too busy working or looking after Theo to think about anything else. But once Theo was in bed, she was very aware of being on her own. How wonderful it would be if there was someone to share these hours.

Unbidden, a face sprang to mind and her mouth thinned. There had never been any question of Ben sharing her life, as he had made clear. Although she may have viewed their affair as the start of something, Ben hadn't seen it that way. One mention of a baby and he had run for the hills and she, for one, wasn't going to try and change his mind. Benedict Legrange had had his chance to be a father and he wasn't going to get a second one!

The sound of the phone ringing cut through her thoughts. Emily ran downstairs and snatched up the receiver before it could wake Theo. 'Emily Jackson.'

'Emily, it's Tom. I'm sorry to bother you but search and rescue have just phoned. Mitch Johnson at The Ship has reported a couple of his guests are missing. Apparently, they told Mitch they were going for a walk along the coastal path this morning and would be back around three but they haven't appeared. Search and rescue are sending a team out to look for them.'

'What do you want me to do?' Emily asked immediately.

'We were wondering if we could use your house as our base. There's no reception for mobile phones once you're on the path and we may need access to a phone,' Tom explained.

'Of course. I'm happy to help any way I can.'

They sorted out the arrangements before she hung up. Emily hurried into the kitchen and filled the kettle. Although it was a warm night, she knew the men would welcome a cup of tea before they set off. The vehicles arrived ten minutes later, two four-by-fours carrying both the team and their equipment. Emily went outside to meet them, standing aside while Tom climbed out of the back of the lead vehicle.

'I see you got drafted in to help,' she said, smiling at him.

'We both did.' Tom stepped aside and she felt her stomach lurch when she saw the man who had got out of the car behind him. 'You remember Ben, don't you? He offered to come along and help.'

'I…erm…yes, of course,' she replied numbly.

'Emily.'

Ben nodded politely although she was aware that he didn't claim that it was good to see her. Why should he, she thought bitterly as she went back inside to make the tea. She must be the last person Ben wanted to see… Correction: she and *Theo* must be the last people he wanted to see, so why should he pretend anything different? Ben had made it abundantly clear that he wasn't interested in sparing her feelings the last time they'd met!

The thought was just what she needed to get back on track. Emily made the tea and loaded the mugs onto a tray. The men were working out a route when she took the drinks outside and they let out a resounding cheer when they saw what she had brought for them. Alan

Parker, the leader of the team, put his arm round her shoulders and gave her a squeeze.

'Atta girl! If I wasn't happily married then I'd propose to you. There's nothing like a woman who knows how to treat a man right!'

Emily laughed as she put the tray on the bonnet of the Land Rover. 'Good job I didn't fetch out the cake as well or who knows what could have happened.'

Everyone laughed, everyone apart from Ben, that was. Emily felt a shiver run through her when she saw the contemptuous look he gave her. His dark brown eyes were filled with scorn, his beautiful mouth curling at the corners with disdain. She didn't need to ask him what was wrong when it was perfectly clear. Ben thought that she was deliberately currying favour with the men, trying to charm them for some reasons of her own. The thought was like a red rag to the proverbial bull. She didn't pause to think as she rounded on him.

'Obviously, you're not susceptible to my offer of tea and cake, Dr Legrange?'

'No.' He gave a very Gallic shrug. 'I am not easily influenced, Miss Jackson.'

'Really?' Emily could hear the challenge in her voice although she knew that she should let the matter drop. However, she'd spent best part of the day worrying about Ben and she was in no mood to compromise. 'That does surprise me.'

'*Oui?* Why is that?' His tone had deepened, sounding richer, darker and ever so slightly threatening, and Emily felt a little thrill run through her because she had managed to get under his skin.

'Oh, just that I find most men are susceptible to a woman's wiles—if she knows what she's doing, of course.'

She smiled sweetly when everyone laughed. It was obvious that the others thought she was teasing but she and Ben knew the truth. Ben might not have wanted her in his life, long term, but for a short time at least he'd wanted *her*. He'd wanted her in his bed, in his arms, and wanted her with a raw, unbridled passion too. He could deny it all he liked but they both knew the truth: when they'd made love, Ben had never thought about anyone else but her.

Ben made his way from the group. Tom was talking to Alan Parker, working out the best route to take, and didn't notice him leaving. Although he knew that he should offer whatever help he could, it was beyond him at that moment. All he could think about was Emily lying in his arms, her face flushed with passion, her body naked to his gaze. Her eyes were half closed, her lips parted, her light brown hair tumbling around her face....

'*Merde!*' The oath tore from his lips before he could stop it and his hands clenched. He wasn't used to losing control but that was how he felt—raw and aching and out of control. It would take very little to give in to the anger that was simmering inside him and that was the last thing he could afford to do.

He wouldn't allow her to get under his skin, wouldn't let her hurt him any more than she had done already. She was a liar and a cheat. She had tried to dupe him into accepting her child as his own. She'd probably slept with him, in fact, for that very purpose. The thought should have been enough to stop him feeling anything but contempt for her yet it didn't. Even now, even knowing what she was capable of, he still wanted her!

'Right, we're all sorted. You and I are going to check out one of the side paths.'

Tom came over to him and Ben hurriedly smoothed his features into something resembling a normal expression. '*Bon*. Do we need to take anything with us—ropes, medical equipment, things like that?'

'Everything we need's in here.' Tom showed him one of the backpacks the team carried. 'It's just basics—torch, whistle, saline, dressings, etcetera. If we do come across the missing couple then we'll contact the rest of the party and go from there.'

He held up a shortwave radio receiver and Ben nodded. 'You said that our phones won't work in this area.'

'No. Reception is patchy throughout this part of Devon. There are plans to build a new transmitter but who knows when it will happen? We'll have to rely on the radio or come back here to Emily's if that's a viable alternative,' Tom explained. 'It's lucky she lives here, isn't it?'

'Hmm.' Ben smiled but he could feel his insides churning again as he glanced towards the cottage. Emily was collecting up the dirty mugs. She bent down to pick up one that had been left on the ground and he felt his breath catch when he was treated to a glimpse of her shapely derrière clad in well-washed denim. He turned away, not wanting to test out his new-found determination to ignore her.

'There isn't a problem with you and Emily, is there?' Tom swung the backpack over his shoulder as he led the way to the footpath.

'A problem?' Ben reiterated to give himself time to think. Although Tom was his closest friend, he had never confided in him about what had gone on and had no intention of doing so. Quite frankly, he wouldn't want anyone to know what a fool he'd been.

'Hmm. I couldn't help noticing a certain vibe between you two just now.' Tom glanced at him as he cleared the stile. 'Tell me to mind my own business, but did something happen between you and Emily when you stayed here the last time?'

'Nothing of any importance,' Ben said lightly. He glanced along the path. 'Is it straight ahead or do we need to turn off?'

'Straight ahead.'

Tom took the hint and didn't say anything else. However, it was worrying to know that his friend had picked up on the atmosphere between him and Emily. As they made their way along the path, Ben promised himself that it would be the first and the last time he made that mistake. From now on he would treat Emily as she deserved to be treated, as someone who didn't feature in his life.

It was just gone ten when the sound of footsteps outside woke Emily. She sat up, groaning when she felt the crick in her neck. Falling asleep on the sofa definitely wasn't a good idea but she'd been loath to go to bed in case she was needed. Now she hurried to the door and flung it open, gasping when she saw Ben helping a middle-aged woman up the path.

'This is Louise. Can she wait here until the rest of the group catches up with us?' he asked briefly.

'Of course!' Emily hurried forward and put her arm around the woman's waist. She flinched when her hand encountered Ben's but there was no way she could remove it when the poor woman needed her support. They helped her inside and got her settled on the sofa. Ben stepped back as soon as Louise was comfortable, his face impassive, but Emily could tell from the tightening of his jaw that he'd enjoyed the contact no more than she had done.

The thought was strangely upsetting. Emily turned away, reluctant to let him see how she felt. 'I'll fetch a blanket. She feels cold despite the fact it's warm outside.'

'Shock,' Ben replied succinctly, crouching down in front of the woman. He gently chafed her hands. 'Her husband fell down the bank of a stream and injured his leg. She was unable to get him out.'

'How is he?' Emily asked, sotto voce, and he shook his head.

'Not too good.'

Emily didn't ask anything else, not wanting to add to the poor woman's distress. Ben asked if he could use the phone to call search and rescue headquarters so she showed him where it was then ran upstairs to fetch a blanket. He was still on the phone when she went back down so she took the blanket through to the sitting room and draped it over Louise then smiled at her. 'I'm going to make you a cup of tea. It will help to warm you up.'

Louise didn't respond. Her face was completely blank as she stared straight ahead. Emily frowned as she headed to the kitchen. Ben had finished his call and she beckoned him over, waiting until they were out of earshot before speaking. 'Has she said anything to you?'

'No. She's not said a word since we found her.' He sighed as he rested his lean frame against the work-top. 'It was sheer luck that we came across them. Tom just happened to glance down the banking and spotted Louise's red jumper. She was just sitting there, not shouting or anything, just cradling her husband's head in her lap.'

'The poor soul!' Emily exclaimed. 'She must have been terrified.'

'*Oui*. To see the one you love in trouble and not be able to help them…!'

Once again he gave that very Gallic shrug and Emily looked away. It was one of the things she remembered most, the way he punctuated his conversation with various gestures. Although Ben's English was faultless thanks to his having an English mother, his French heritage from his father was still very apparent and had always been a huge part of his charm. That along with so many other things, of course.

She closed her mind to that stupid thought as she made the tea. She filled a mug, adding both milk and sugar. Ben smiled faintly as he watched her.

'Ah, the British answer to all life's ills—hot sweet tea.'

'It's very reviving,' she countered.

'Oh, it is. I learned that for myself when I first came here. Ros would make me a cup of tea and all of a sudden everything seemed that bit brighter.'

'Sadly it can't cure everything. There are some problems that can't be solved by a cup of tea.' She hadn't meant to say that, certainly hadn't intended to allude to their problem, his refusal to acknowledge their child, and bit her lip. Ben's expression darkened as he stared at her with undisguised contempt.

'Some problems are too huge to be resolved. It needs trust and honesty to sort out important issues. When they are absent, there is never a way forward.'

He went back to the sitting room, leaving her to stew that over. Emily ground her teeth, hating the fact that he had the gall to make out that *she* was lacking in honesty. Picking up the mug, she hurried after him, hating him with every fibre of her being. Ben had been so afraid of facing up to his responsibilities that he had chosen to deny his own child. There couldn't be anything more dishonest than that!

CHAPTER THREE

Tom arrived about twenty minutes later. Emily hurried to the door when she heard his footsteps coming up the path. The rest of the team were assembling by the cars while Alan supervised the loading of the stretcher into one of the vehicles.

'How is he?' Emily asked, ushering Tom inside.

'Not too good.' He glanced into the sitting room and sighed. 'Severe hypothermia from being half-submerged in the stream for several hours, plus a badly fractured femur. Good job Ben spoke to HQ. They've arranged for the helicopter to meet us in town and do the transfer.'

Emily nodded, not needing to labour the point. Speed was of the essence and the poor man was already at a disadvantage after being missing for so long. She led the way into the sitting room, avoiding Ben's eyes as she went over to Louise. She'd let Tom fill him in. The less she had to say to him the better.

'Louise, your husband is going to be flown to hospital in the emergency helicopter,' she explained gently, sitting down beside her. 'There isn't room for you,

I'm afraid, but someone will take you there so you can be with him.'

'Alan's going to take her,' Tom put in, dropping wearily into an armchair.

'Oh, that's good.' Emily smiled at the woman but still failed to get a response. Louise continued to sit there. She hadn't attempted to drink her tea despite Emily's urgings and Emily was beginning to feel really concerned.

'Louise seems to be very shocked,' she said, glancing at Tom. 'She hasn't said a word since she got here.'

Tom frowned. 'She didn't say anything when we found her, either.' He turned to Ben. 'Do you think this is a normal reaction?'

'It's difficult to say. Everyone reacts differently to stress,' Ben replied. He got up and came over to the sofa and Emily hurriedly moved aside as he crouched down in front of the woman. 'Do you understand what we are saying, Louise? Your husband is alive and he's being taken to hospital.'

Louise looked at him with hollow eyes. 'Are you sure? Sure that Dennis is alive? Only the last time it happened, they were wrong, you see.'

Emily frowned. 'The last time? You mean this has happened before?'

'Not to Dennis, no. But to my first husband...' Louise broke off. She gave a little sob then managed to collect herself. 'Frank and I were out shopping one day when he had a heart attack. The paramedics told me that he was all right but he wasn't. I don't think they meant to lie, really, they just didn't realise...'

Louise couldn't go on as tears overwhelmed her. Emily patted her hand, trying to hide her dismay. No wonder the poor woman was so distressed. To have it happen once would have been bad enough but to have something similar occur a second time must be horrendous.

'It isn't the same this time,' Ben said gently and Emily shivered when she heard the compassion in his voice. Nobody hearing it could doubt that he wanted to help and she suddenly wished with all her heart that she'd received this kind of consideration when she had told him about Theo. It was hard not to let her emotions get the better of her as he continued in the same caring tone.

'Your husband is alive and he will be treated at the hospital. Yes, he is very sick, but he's alive, Louise, and everything possible will be done to keep him that way.'

Louise took a shuddering breath then stumbled to her feet. 'I want to see him.'

'I'll take you,' Tom offered immediately, standing up. He led her to the door, leaving Emily alone with Ben. He stood up as well, making it clear that he had no intention of lingering. Why should he, Emily thought bitterly as she followed him out. There was nothing here to interest him, after all.

'Mummy!'

A pitiful wail from the top of the stairs brought her spinning round and her heart sank when she saw Theo standing there. He had Raffie, his favourite toy giraffe clutched in one hand, and his comfort blanket in the other. Obviously all the comings and goings had woken him up.

'It's all right, darling,' she said, running up the stairs and picking him up. She cuddled him close, feeling the tremor that passed through his sturdy little body. The cottage was quite secluded and he wasn't used to hearing a lot of strange noises during the night.

She carried him downstairs, knowing it was pointless taking him back to bed. Theo needed a little reassurance and there was no one better for that than his mummy. She reached the last tread and stopped, only then realising that Ben was still standing where she'd left him. She'd expected him to beat a hasty retreat as soon as he'd heard Theo but, oddly enough, he was still there.

She glanced at him and felt her blood freeze when she saw the expression on his face. Shock, disbelief, amazement were all etched there clear to see. For a moment Emily couldn't understand what was going on and then it struck her in a blinding flash what had happened. Ben had finally been forced to acknowledge the truth. Now that he'd seen Theo, he could no longer claim he wasn't the child's father. The resemblance which had been so apparent to her from the moment her son had been born couldn't be denied, although no doubt once Ben recovered his composure, he would do so. Tipping back her head, she looked him straight in the eyes.

'This is my son, Theo.'

Ben felt as though his body had turned to jelly. His legs were shaking and his insides were trembling as he stared at the little boy clinging hold of Emily's neck. The resemblance was unmistakable. He had two nephews and this child—Theo?—looked so like them that it was staggering. Had he been wrong? Was it possible that he had fathered this child after all?

'Right, that's settled. Alan's taking Louise with him...' Tom came back into the cottage. He stopped when he realised that he was interrupting something. He glanced uncertainly from Emily and Theo to Ben then did a double take, and Ben knew—he just knew!— that Tom had seen it too, seen the resemblance between him and Emily's son.

It was all too much to take in and far too much to deal with. Swinging round, Ben strode out of the door, hearing Emily's murmured response when Tom said something to her before he quickly followed him. He got into the back of the second Land Rover, cramming himself into the corner as Tom got in beside him. The rest of the team had divided themselves between the vehicles as best they could with the stretcher taking up so much room. It was a squeeze to fit everyone in but he didn't care. At least Tom couldn't ask him any awkward questions, awkward because he had no idea what the answers were. Had he been mistaken, had he seen something in the child that wasn't there? Maybe he could have convinced himself if his friend hadn't seen it too!

The drive back to town was completed in silence, at least on their behalf. The rest of the group was buoyed up by the fact that they'd found the missing couple. They tried to persuade him and Tom to join them for a celebratory pint at The Ship but Ben refused. He needed to be on his own, needed to sort out how he felt and after that, more importantly, he needed to work out what he was going to do. If the child *was* his then his whole life was about to change.

'How about a nightcap?' Tom let them in, closing the door quietly so as not to disturb Hannah and Charlie who were asleep upstairs. 'You look as though you could do with one, if you don't mind me saying so.'

'Feel free.' Ben sighed as he followed Tom into the sitting room. Maybe he would prefer to be alone but he could hardly refuse to talk to Tom. Slumping down in a chair, he looked at his friend with sardonic amusement. 'It's been an eventful night, one way and another.'

'It has indeed.' Tom handed him a glass of single malt then sat down. 'Am I right in thinking that tonight turned out to be rather a shock for you?'

'Yes.' Ben took a sip of the fiery liquid and let it trickle down his throat.

'So you had no idea about Theo?'

'Yes and no.' Another sip of whisky followed the first and the fire reached his belly. He had a son, a child of his own, something he had never dared hope he would have. Shock slowly started to turn to something more, the first glimmer of a far more positive emotion, but he battened it down. He didn't want to get ahead of himself, didn't want to believe the evidence of his eyes with nothing to back it up.

'Yes and no? I don't understand. Either you knew that Theo was yours or you didn't. Which is it?'

'Emily told me she was expecting my child but I didn't believe her.' The words sounded so bald that the burgeoning feeling of euphoria disappeared. They obviously had a detrimental effect on Tom too because his tone sharpened.

'Why the hell not? Emily's not the sort of woman who'd string a guy along. Anyone who knows her will tell you that.'

Ben grimaced, aware that he had sunk more than a little in his friend's estimation. 'I didn't believe her because I thought I was incapable of fathering a child.'

'Really? How come?'

Tom's tone was less abrasive and Ben sighed. Although he rarely talked about what had happened this was one time when he needed to open up.

'I had Hodgkin's lymphoma when I was in my twenties.' He shrugged. 'I had chemotherapy and I was told that it was unlikely I would be able to father a child because of the combination of drugs I'd received. A subsequent fertility test seemingly proved that.'

'I had no idea!' Tom exclaimed.

Ben smiled wryly. 'It's not something I talk about normally.'

'No. I can understand that.' Tom frowned. 'So, what you're saying is that you've always believed you were infertile?'

Ben nodded. 'Yes. When Emily came to see me in Paris, I simply assumed she was lying and that the child wasn't mine.'

'But surely you knew her well enough to know that she wouldn't do something like that?' Tom protested.

'Maybe I should have done. However, when you have always believed what you've been told, it's difficult to accept that someone is telling you something very different.' Ben summoned a smile, trying not to let his friend see how awful he felt. He had been so cruel to Emily that day, turned her away with harsh words instead of offering her the support she'd deserved. He couldn't bear to think how she must have suffered.

'I suppose so.'

Tom sounded dubious and Ben realised that his friend still considered him to be at fault in some way. The fact that he felt he was too didn't make him feel any better. They both drank a little more whisky before Tom spoke again and there was a definite challenge in his voice.

'So what are you going to do? Are you going to try and sort out this mess or are you planning on leaving the situation as it is?'

'Obviously, it needs sorting out. If I'm Theo's father then there is no way that I intend to turn my back on him. I want to be involved in his life.'

'If Emily will let you.'

'*Oui*. If Emily will let me,' Ben agreed flatly. 'I would not blame her if she refused. When I recall what I said to her that day…' He broke off and shrugged.

Tom shook his head. 'It seems to me that you've a lot of ground to make up. If I can help in any way then just ask. However, I have a feeling that only you can work this out, you and Emily, that is.' Tom downed the rest of his drink and stood up. He patted Ben on the shoulder as he passed. 'Why don't you sleep on it? Most problems appear better after a night's rest, I find.'

Ben stayed where he was as Tom headed upstairs. He swirled the whisky around the glass. Would there be a solution in the morning though? Would he know how to approach Emily and make his apologies? Would she accept them? He had accused her of lying about something so important and he wouldn't blame her if she refused to have anything to do with him. Tom was right because he should have realised that Emily would never try to deceive him that way. Even though they had known each other for such a short time, he should have recognized that it was alien to her nature.

He sighed. In his own defence, he had firmly believed that he was infertile. Although, as a doctor, he understood that nothing was ever one hundred per cent certain, the tests he'd had seemingly had ruled out the possibility of him fathering a child. That was why it had never occurred to him that Emily might have been telling him the truth. He had *seen* the test results, *seen* the evidence with his own eyes, ergo she'd been lying.

The fact that he'd felt so hurt and betrayed by her apparent treachery had been another reason why he had reacted so strongly, he realised. Having cancer had changed his whole outlook on life. He had stopped planning for the future for the simple reason that the future might never happen. That was why he had taken only short-term working contracts after he'd recovered. A month here, two months there—it may not have been the career he'd planned, but at least he wouldn't end up letting people down.

As for his private life, well, that had been simpler; any relationships he'd had had been strictly casual. There were no certainties in his life any more. Things could and did change in the blink of an eye as he knew from experience. He wasn't in a position whereby he could commit himself to a relationship. However, when he'd met Emily, he had found himself doing the unthinkable, imagining what it would be like to share his life with her. That was why it had hit him so hard when she'd told him she was pregnant. He had always wanted a child and he'd known that he would have loved their child so very much…

Ben made himself stop right there. That was all in the past. Now he had to focus on the present, on finding a way to persuade Emily to give him a second chance. He only had to recall his relationship with his own father to understand how important it was that he and Theo got to know one another. It wasn't going to be easy to convince Emily after the way he had behaved. Maybe there had been mitigating factors, and maybe she would take them into account if he was lucky, but all the maybes in the world didn't add up to a guarantee. Whilst he was sure that Theo would benefit from having him around, he doubted if Emily would feel that she'd gain from it.

He grimaced. From what he had seen, Emily neither needed nor wanted him in her life.

Emily was glad that it was Saturday and that there was no surgery that day. Although she loved her job, a sleepless night had left her feeling drained. She got Theo dressed then gave him his breakfast in the garden because it was another gloriously sunny day. Leaving him eating his cereal, she went back inside and made herself a cup of coffee.

All night long thoughts had whizzed around her

head, thoughts of Theo and Ben and what would happen. Would Ben change his mind about wanting to be involved in Theo's life now that he'd seen him, or would it make no difference whatsoever? It would be easier if she knew how she felt about it all but she didn't. On the one hand she didn't want anything to do with Ben after the way he had treated her; however, on the other, she couldn't bear to think that Theo might suffer if she denied him access to his father. Having been brought up by parents who had loved and supported her unconditionally, she didn't want to deny Theo that same opportunity.

A knock on the front door roused her from her reverie and she hurried to answer it, expecting it to be her elderly neighbour, Mrs Rose. She often called on Saturday morning with her shopping list so that Emily could pick up what she needed at the supermarket. Opening the door, she summoned a smile that rapidly faded when she found Ben standing on the step.

'What do you want?' she demanded.

'I think that's obvious, don't you?' he replied calmly.

Emily's lips compressed firstly because the trite answer annoyed her intensely and secondly because how dared he sound so calm when she felt so churned up? 'No, I don't think it's obvious. Not when it concerns a man who has no desire whatsoever to acknowledge his responsibilities.'

'That was then and this is now.' He gave another of those shrugs but it had the opposite effect this time. Emily felt her temper soar. His arrogance was breathtaking. He seemed to think that he could pick and choose what he wanted to do with no recourse to anyone else, and especially not to her!

'Really? Well, I'm afraid it doesn't work like that, Ben. You made your feelings perfectly clear when I came to see you. You didn't believe me when I told you I was expecting your child, or at least, that was the line you fed me.'

'It wasn't a line. I didn't believe you.'

The conviction in his voice cut through her anger and she stared at him in shock. 'You really mean that, don't you?'

'*Oui*. I had no reason to believe what you were saying but every reason to doubt it.' He paused and she sensed that he found it difficult to continue but she refused to help him. Why should she make this easier for him when he had been so cruel to her?

'I had cancer when I was in my twenties. After I'd finished my treatment, I was told that I could never father a child.' He looked her in the eyes and she could see the pain in his. 'That was why I didn't believe you, Emily. I couldn't accept that the child you were carrying was mine when I'd been told it could never happen.'

CHAPTER FOUR

'CANCER!'

Ben could hear the shock in Emily's voice and his heart contracted in sudden dread. The main reason why he avoided mentioning that he'd had cancer was because of the reaction it aroused. People feared cancer more than anything else and their response simply heightened his feeling of vulnerability. Although he'd been effectively cleared of the cancer, the thought that it might return was always at the back of his mind. He knew that his response wasn't unusual; he'd met other cancer survivors and they had felt the same. Not even being told that they were cured could completely remove the last vestiges of fear.

'*Oui*. I had Hodgkin's lymphoma,' he said flatly, not wanting to go down that route. He needed to tell Emily the facts as emotionlessly as possible and see where they went from there. 'It was treated successfully. However, the drugs I was given left me infertile…or so I believed.'

'I don't know what to say.' Emily took a deep breath and he saw a little colour come back to her face. 'Obviously, that does help to explain why you reacted the way you did when I came to see you…'

'Yes, it does!' he said urgently, wondering if this was the opening he needed.

'However, it doesn't excuse it. You never gave me a chance, Ben, never even *considered* the possibility that I was telling you the truth. You'd been told you couldn't father a child so that meant I was lying.' She stared at him and the absence of warmth in her eyes sent a chill through him. 'It proves how little you knew me, how little you cared to know.'

'That's not fair!'

'Isn't it? I disagree. I was just a convenience to you, someone you slept with, someone you never intended to see again once you left here.'

'You make it sound so…so cold blooded,' he protested and she shrugged.

'I'm merely being truthful. We had an affair and that was it. There was never any talk of us staying together, was there?'

'Perhaps we did not discuss it but neither did we rule it out,' he countered and she laughed.

'Oh, well done. I believe that's called thinking on your feet. You don't want to antagonise me so you've decided to put a spin on things.'

'No, I don't want to antagonise you, Emily. It's the last thing I want to do.' The comment had touched a nerve. Maybe there was some truth in what she'd said, but the situation wasn't as clear cut as she believed. Although he may not have been able to offer her more than the few glorious weeks they'd had, it didn't mean he hadn't wanted to.

It was another thought he didn't want to dwell on

and he hurried on. 'I want us to talk, Emily. I want us to try and reach some sort of agreement to help us deal with this situation.'

'And what if I don't want to talk? What if I feel that it would be better for everyone if you went back to Paris and carried on with your life—then what will you do?'

'Try to change your mind, and if that doesn't work, take whatever steps are necessary.' His tone was flat which was surprising when he seemed to be a seething mass of emotions inside. Emily's antipathy couldn't be plainer. That was painful enough, but the fact that it was bound to have an effect on his hopes of building a relationship with Theo made it so much worse.

'I intend to be involved in my son's life whether you like the idea or not. I may be at fault for not believing you were carrying my child but there is nothing I can do about that now except explain my reasons and apologise. However, if you deny me access then I warn you that I shall fight you, Emily.'

Emily felt a rush of panic assail her. She hadn't meant to stir up such a reaction but it seemed she had. She bit her lip, hating the feeling that she'd been backed into a corner. She needed time to think, time to work out how she felt. Learning that Ben had had cancer was a huge shock and she knew that it had made a difference. She needed to get that straight in her head before she did anything else.

'Look, this is all getting out of hand,' she began then stopped when Theo appeared, carrying his empty cereal bowl.

'Finished, Mummy,' he said, handing it to her before looking curiously at the man standing on the step.

Emily felt her heart catch when once again she was made aware of the resemblance between them. With his black curls, olive skin and huge dark eyes, Theo was the image of his father. Ben obviously realised it too because an expression of amazement crossed his face once more.

'*Bonjour*, Theo. How are you today?' he asked softly, bending down. He ran his finger down the little boy's cheek and Emily felt a rush of tears fill her eyes when she saw him shudder. It was the first time Ben had actually touched his son and it was obvious that the contact had affected him deeply. It was only when Theo backed away, sheltering shyly behind her legs, that she collected herself. It was Theo who mattered most. How Ben did or didn't feel wasn't important.

She scooped the little boy into her arms and cuddled him close. Although Theo was a friendly, outgoing child with people he knew, he tended to be wary around strangers and she didn't want him getting upset. She looked Ben firmly in the eyes, determined to start the way she intended to go on. 'I'm sorry but I'm going to have to ask you to leave. I have things to do and I can't spare the time to stand here talking to you.'

'Really?' Ben's expression darkened as he straightened. 'And when will you have the time, Emily?'

'I'm not sure.' She went to close the door, stopping when he put out his hand.

'That's not good enough, I'm afraid. We need to talk and I have no intention of allowing you to fob me off.'

'The way you fobbed me off in Paris,' she shot back and he flinched.

'I have already apologised for that. If you want me to apologise again then I shall. I am very sorry for the way I behaved that day. I was unnecessarily harsh, even though at the time I truly believed I had every right to be.'

The words were faultless; however the tone of his voice told a very different story and her mouth compressed. Ben may be paying lip service to an apology but he didn't really mean it. He still believed that he'd been right to call her a liar and a cheat without taking the time to consider that he might have been wrong. It simply drove it home to her once more how little he had cared about her. She'd been good enough to share his bed but she hadn't warranted his respect. How on earth could they find any common ground with regard to Theo when their relationship was based on such shaky footings?

'This isn't getting us anywhere,' she said quickly, afraid that it would take very little for her to break down. Although she'd been under no illusions about how Ben felt, it hurt to know that he'd cared so little about her when she had cared so much about him. 'I don't want you upsetting Theo so I want you to leave. If you insist on talking to me then I suggest we do it away from here.'

'That's fine by me, although I must point out that I have every intention of seeing Theo again.' His expression softened as he looked at the little boy. 'I want to get to know him, find out what he likes and dislikes.'

'If—and it's a big if at this stage—we reach that point then I won't stand in your way if I think it's best for Theo. However, I won't allow you to bulldoze me into doing what you want, Ben. It's Theo I'm concerned about, not you or what you want.'

'Which is how it should be.'

He stepped away from the door, the sun striking sparks off his black hair. Emily felt her breath catch as she was suddenly reminded of the first time she had seen him. It had been the summer then too and he'd been sitting on the harbour wall, watching the fishing boats unloading their catch. Tom had arranged for him to stay with Simon and Ros while he recuperated from some bug he'd caught whilst working overseas and his skin had been pale beneath its natural olive tan, his dark eyes slightly sunken, but he'd still been the most attractive man she had ever seen. She had recently ended a relationship and had returned to Bride's Bay where she had grown up to start afresh, never expecting that she would meet someone like him.

They had started talking, inconsequential chatter about the weather, and things had progressed from there. Within a week they'd become lovers; by the end of a month she had known she was in love with him. Maybe that was why it had turned out so badly, she thought. It had happened too fast, the emotions they'd felt—or what she'd *thought* they had felt—had been too fierce. However, Emily knew that she would never experience anything like it again, that no matter who she met in the future she would never feel for him even a fraction of what she had felt for Ben during that brief glorious summer.

Her heart ached as she watched him drive away. It felt as though all the wonderful memories of that time they'd had together had gone with him. Maybe it had been foolish to hold them in her heart after what had happened but she'd never quite been able to erase them. She had drawn comfort from remembering how much fun they'd had and how wonderful their lovemaking had been. Now they were gone and in their place there was an emptiness that it would be impossible to fill.

Ben had never loved her. He had never truly cared about her. Not even a million memories of sunny days and laughter could make up for those cold, hard facts.

Ben drove back to Tom and Hannah's house, aware that he hadn't handled the situation well. He'd been determined to get things sorted out but he had achieved very little. So Emily had agreed that she would allow him to see Theo but only as long as she felt it was in the child's best interests. Although Ben knew she was right to take such a stance, he could feel his frustration mounting. It could take years before she allowed him proper access to the child, years neither he nor Theo could afford to lose. He needed to convince her that Theo would benefit from having him around and he needed to do it fast!

He let himself into the cottage, doing his best to fix a cheerful expression to his face. However, Tom took one look at him when he walked into the garden and rolled his eyes.

'Hmm, you don't look too happy. Do I take it that you've been to see Emily?'

'How did you guess?' Ben dropped into a deck chair and sighed. 'She didn't exactly welcome me with open arms, shall we say.'

'And do you blame her?'

Tom's tone was acerbic and Ben laughed shortly. 'You don't pull your punches, *mon ami.*'

'I'm a realist. Oh, I know you had your reasons for believing that Emily was telling you a pack of lies, but it must have been truly awful for her. She's not going to forgive or forget what you did overnight.'

'*Non.* And that's what worries me.' Ben shrugged when Tom looked at him. 'I don't want to wait years to get to know my son. He needs me now, not when Emily decides the time is right.'

'We understand how you feel but you can't rush these things, Ben,' Hannah put in gently. 'Look at it from Emily's point of view. You hurt her—badly. Why should she let you back into her life when you may very well hurt Theo as well?'

'Impossible!' Ben reared up in the chair, stung by the accusation. 'I would never, ever hurt that child!'

'You know that but Emily doesn't.' Hannah held up her hand when he went to protest. 'She only has past events to go on and, let's face it, you didn't exactly cover yourself in glory, did you?'

'No. I didn't.' Ben subsided into the chair. 'I never even considered the fact that she might be telling me the truth. I just assumed she was using me.' He shrugged, hoping it wasn't apparent how much it had hurt to think that. He had truly believed that Emily had felt something for him, so to discover that he'd been merely a means to an end had been unbearably painful.

'And now you know that she wasn't using you,' Tom said bluntly. 'She was telling you the truth.'

'Yes.'

Ben stood up, too wound up to sit there while they discussed the matter. Little Charlie was playing in his sandpit and he wandered over to him, kneeling down so he could help the child fill his bucket with sand. Would he get the chance to play like this with Theo? he wondered. He hoped so, hoped he could persuade Emily to see sense and not make him wait too long. He was due back at the clinic next week which gave him just five days to convince her. It wasn't very long yet he had a feeling that if he couldn't do it in that time, he never would. He had to make Emily see that he could be trusted, that despite how he'd behaved in the past, he would never let her and Theo down.

He stood up, feeling a sudden unease run through him. When had it become as important to be there for Emily as it was to be there for his son? He wasn't sure but he could no longer separate the two. They were locked together in his mind and he wanted to take care of both of them.

If Emily would let him.

Tuesday arrived bringing with it the start of the working week after the bank holiday hiatus. Emily dropped Theo at nursery and headed to the surgery. The weather had changed that day and there were dark clouds scudding across the sky when she let herself in. Lizzie had the kettle on and she looked round when Emily appeared.

'I take it you'd like a cuppa?'

'Please.' Emily shed her jacket and shivered. 'It's a bit chilly this morning, isn't it?'

'It is, although I don't suppose we can grumble after the weekend we had.' Lizzie handed her a mug and grinned at her. 'Have you seen Ben? He was at Tom and Hannah's barbecue on Saturday night. He looked great, too, miles better than the last time I saw him.'

'Hmm, yes, I've seen him,' Emily mumbled, using her tea as an excuse not to say anything else.

Ben had been constantly on her mind. The thought of him having had cancer had hit her hard, far harder than she would have expected. She kept thinking about how awful it must have been for him to know that his life was hanging in the balance. Although he had said that it had been treated successfully, she wasn't sure if that meant he had been cured or was in remission. She shivered. That was another thought that had played on her mind. What would happen if the cancer returned? Was there more treatment he could have?

'Of course you have! Tom mentioned something about them using your house as a base when they were looking for that couple who went missing,' Lizzie said happily, oblivious to any undercurrents. 'I saw Mitch Johnson on my way in and he'd been to the hospital to see them. The chap's on the mend apparently, which is good news.'

'It is,' Emily agreed then glanced round when she heard footsteps crossing Reception. 'It's a bit early for people to be arriving,' she began then stopped when Ben appeared.

'Good morning. I hope I'm not disturbing you.' He smiled at them but Emily could sense a certain tension about him which immediately put her on her guard.

'Simon's not come through from the house yet,' she informed him sharply. 'Go on through. I'm sure he'll be pleased to see you.'

'He knows I'm coming.' He shrugged, his broad shoulders moving lightly beneath the thin cotton shirt.

Emily looked away when she felt her stomach give a familiar little lurch. Ben had always had this effect on her right from the beginning. All it took was the slightest gesture, the lightest touch, and she responded. Whilst that may have been acceptable three years ago, it certainly wasn't something she relished now.

'Really?' she replied coolly, so coolly that she saw Lizzie look at her in surprise.

'*Oui*. We arranged it on Saturday at the barbecue.' Ben's tone was equally cool but there was an undercurrent to it that made her heart race. She had a feeling that she wasn't going to like where this was leading, yet she was powerless to stop it.

'Simon was telling me about this new health centre they're building and the problems he's had finding the time to meet with the architects, etcetera.' He smiled faintly. 'I understand how difficult it is because I went through the same thing when we were building the clinic in Paris. There was never enough time to fit everything in.'

'This is all very interesting but I really do need to

get on.' Emily put down her cup, ignoring Lizzie's gasp. Maybe she was being rude but there was no way that she could stand there any longer. Just being around Ben was a big enough strain but to have to make conversation as well…

'Of course. I'm sorry. I didn't mean to hold you up.' Another smile drifted her way although there was little warmth in it and she shivered. 'I just wanted you to know that I shall be working here for the next few days. It will give Simon a breathing space so that he can catch up.'

'What!' Emily exclaimed. 'You're going to be working here?'

'*Oui*. It's the least I can do after everything he and Ros did for me three years ago.' His voice dropped, sounding so rich and deep that the tiny hairs all over her body stood to attention. 'My life would have turned out very differently if they hadn't invited me to stay with them. It is strange how these things work out, isn't it, Emily?'

CHAPTER FIVE

'IT's impetigo, Mrs Barnes. It's highly contagious so I'm afraid you will have to keep Josh off school until it clears up.' Ben smiled soothingly at the woman seated in front of the desk but staying calm obviously wasn't on her agenda.

'Off school? But he only goes back tomorrow after the summer holidays!' Maxine Barnes glared at the unhappy seven-year-old. The area around his nose and mouth was a mass of tiny, weeping blisters. 'Now see what you've done? I told you to stop picking your nose, didn't I?'

Ben bit back a sigh when the child started to cry. Some people really shouldn't have children, he thought, as he passed a box of tissues across the desk. The thought reminded him of Theo and he felt his heart lift. Maybe he shouldn't have been able to father a child but he wasn't sorry it had happened, despite the problems.

'It isn't Josh's fault, Mrs Barnes. The bacteria that cause impetigo enter the skin through a cut or a cold sore, or even a patch of eczema. It's very easy for a child to catch it.'

'Hmph.' Maxine Barnes didn't look convinced and

he didn't try to persuade her. He printed out a script for antibiotics and handed it to her.

'This should clear it up. Use the cream three times a day and wash off any loose crusts with soap and water. It's highly contagious, as I said, so Josh will need his own towel and face flannel. They will need to be boiled after they've been used as will his bedding to avoid passing on the infection. Have you any more children at home?'

'Five,' Maxine said, standing up. She glared at Ben as though he were to blame. 'So I don't know where you think I'll get the time to be boiling bedding. I'm run off my feet as it is!'

She stormed out without another word and certainly not a thank-you. Ben grimaced as he got up to wash his hands. He'd not exactly won her over, had he? That made two women he'd managed to upset in under an hour.

He sighed as he dried his hands on a paper towel. Emily's reaction to the news that he'd be working at the surgery had been nothing less than he'd expected, yet it had still stung. She had made it clear that he was the last person she wanted to be around and he couldn't help comparing how she felt now to how she'd felt three years ago. Back then, she'd made no secret of the fact that she had enjoyed his company and it was painful to know how much her opinion of him had changed.

'I'm sorry to interrupt you, but I need a word about a patient.'

Ben felt his heart lurch when he looked round and saw Emily standing in the doorway. She was dressed in her customary working attire which comprised a navy blue cotton tunic with matching navy blue trousers yet he couldn't help thinking how much the outfit suited her, emphasising the rounded fullness of her breasts and the trimness of her waist. Her light brown hair was drawn back from her face and held at her nape with a tortoiseshell clip, and he felt a little flurry run through him when he found himself remembering how it looked when it was loose. How many times had he woken to see her hair spread across his pillow? How many times had he buried his face in its softness? He'd never allowed himself to remember things like that before, yet all of a sudden the memories were as sharp and as clear as ever.

'Of course.' Ben adopted a carefully neutral expression as he returned to the desk. He couldn't afford to let Emily know what he was thinking in case it jeopardised his plans for Theo. He must be the last person she wanted lusting after her after the way he had behaved! 'What can I do for you?'

'I've got a woman with me who's presenting with all the symptoms of angina—chest pains, sweating, dizziness. She's staying here on holiday and woke up this morning feeling very unwell.' Emily shrugged. 'Lizzie asked me to have a look at her, but I really think she needs to be seen by a doctor.'

'And you've tried Tom and Hannah but they're busy,' Ben put in wryly.

'Yes.' She didn't prevaricate and he swallowed his sigh. If it were up to Emily then he wouldn't have been consulted at all.

'In that case, I'd better take a look at her. Do you
want to fetch her through here or shall I come with you?'

'You'd better come through to my room,' she said
stiffly, turning to leave.

Ben caught her up in the corridor, moderating his
pace as they made their way to the opposite end of the
building where Emily had her room. She paused outside
the door and he could tell that she was deliberately putting up a barrier between them. Emily wasn't prepared
to give an inch which made his task all the harder but he
wasn't going to be deterred, if that's what she hoped. He
would be a proper father to Theo whether she liked it or
not, although he really and truly hoped that she would.

'The patient's name is Helen Scott. She's fifty-two
years old and recently widowed,' she informed him before opening the door.

'Thank you,' Ben said quietly as he followed her in.
He would get nowhere if he pushed her. He had to give
her time and hope that he could win her round. At least
by working here, they would be in daily contact for
the next week, which was why he had offered his help.
Hopefully, the time he spent at the surgery would lay
the groundwork for their future relationship.

The fact that there was no guarantee his plan would
work worried him but he pushed the thought aside as he
went over to the couch. 'Hello, Mrs Scott, I'm Benedict
Legrange. I'm covering for one of the doctors here.
Emily tells me that you aren't feeling very well.'

'No, I'm not, Doctor.'

Helen summoned a smile but Ben could tell the effort
it cost her. He sat down on the edge of the couch and

checked her pulse, preferring to do it the old-fashioned way rather than use the machine. Although it was rather rapid, it wasn't worryingly so, and he smiled at her. 'Your pulse is a little fast but that's understandable. Emily told me that you have pains in your chest. Where about does it hurt exactly?'

'Just here.' Helen touched the centre of her chest.

'And how bad is it on a scale of one to five, with one being the least severe and five being the worst?' He knew that Emily was listening, but he did his best to block out everything except his patient. There would be time enough to worry about Emily later.

'I don't know… I've not had a pain like this before,' Helen said uncertainly.

'So this is the first time it's happened?' Ben queried.

'Yes.' Helen bit her lip and he could tell that she was struggling to hold back her tears.

He patted her hand. 'Take your time, Helen. We're here to help you.'

'I know. It's just that it's so hard…'

Tears began to stream down her face and Emily stepped forward. She bent down and put her arm around the other woman's shoulders. 'Is there anyone we can call, Helen? A friend or a family member, perhaps?'

'No, there's no one. I'm here on my own. It's my first holiday since Richard died and I wish I hadn't come now!'

Ben moved out of the way so that Emily could take his place. She was so good with people, he thought, as he watched her, genuinely kind and caring. How had he ever imagined that she would try to trick him?

The guilt he felt was more than he could handle right then. Walking over to the desk, he phoned Lizzie and asked her if she would mind making a cup of tea for their patient. It arrived a few minutes later and he thanked her warmly before carrying it over to the couch.

'Here you are. I have it on good authority that a cup of tea works wonders,' he said with a smile.

'Thank you.' Helen smiled shakily as she accepted the cup. Emily looked up and Ben felt his heart lift when he saw the approval in her eyes. Maybe it was foolish, but it felt good to know that he'd done something right for once.

By the time Helen had finished her tea, she seemed a lot better. Emily took the cup off her and put it on the desk. She couldn't fault the way Ben had handled the situation, she thought, glancing at him. He had been both kind and patient, taking his time as he had reassured Helen. He had been exactly the same the night he had brought that missing walker to her house and she had to admit that she was impressed. The thought was disquieting bearing in mind that she wasn't looking for things to admire about him. But it was obvious that Ben genuinely cared…or, at least, he cared about his patients, she amended. When it came to anyone else, it was a very different matter.

The memory of how he had treated her in Paris was still very raw. Emily forced it from her mind as he sat down beside the couch. Maybe she would be able to forgive him in time but not at the moment.

'You said that you hadn't had pain like this before,

Helen, so do you know what caused it today?' Ben asked. 'Were you doing something strenuous perhaps?'

'Not at all. I'd just made myself some breakfast when it started,' Helen explained. 'I've rented a cottage near Denton's Cove and all I've been doing for the past week is reading and walking.'

'How far do you walk each day?' Ben said quickly.

'Oh, not far. Just a couple of miles, if that.' She sighed. 'Richard was a keen walker. He used to go out for the whole day but I never went with him. He used to tease me about it, said my legs would stop working if I didn't use them more!'

Ben laughed. 'But he didn't manage to convince you?'

'No. I prefer my comforts, I'm afraid,' Helen replied, smiling. She looked so much better that Emily was amazed by the change in her.

'How long is it since your husband died?' Ben enquired gently.

'Six months next week,' Helen replied, her smile fading.

'I imagine it must be very difficult for you,' he continued. 'It sounds as though you and your husband had a wonderful relationship.'

Emily frowned, unsure if it was wise to raise the subject when Helen was looking so much better.

'We did. We were married for almost thirty years and I miss him so much,' Helen admitted, her voice catching.

'I'm sure you do. It takes time to get over losing

someone you love, Helen. I have a feeling that you haven't really given yourself time to grieve, have you?'

'I try not to give in to it,' Helen confessed. 'I don't want the children to see me crying. Oh, I know they're grown up now but I still worry about them. The last thing I want is them finding me crying my eyes out.'

'I understand, but it doesn't help to bottle up your feelings.' Ben's tone was firm. 'It could be that the pain and everything else you've experienced today was caused by stress. You've been trying so hard to hold it all together for the sake of your family and now that you've taken some time for yourself, your body is rebelling.'

'Do you really think so?' Helen asked in surprise.

'I think it's possible, although I am not ruling out any other causes at this stage which is why I want to send you to the hospital for an ECG. That will show if there's anything wrong with your heart.'

'I've always been extremely fit,' Helen protested and he nodded.

'I'm sure you have. However, I'd feel happier if you'd have the ECG. I'd also like you to make an appointment with your own GP when you return home. He may want to do some blood tests to check on your general health.'

'Well, if you think I should, Dr Legrange,' Helen agreed reluctantly.

'I do. It would also be a good idea if you had counselling to help you deal with your loss. Your GP should be able to give you details of any groups offering bereavement counselling in your area. You may not feel that you need it, but it can help enormously so I hope you'll think about it.'

He gave her his most winning smile and Emily sighed when she saw the older woman immediately melt. Few women could resist when Ben turned on the charm, she thought wryly. She certainly hadn't been able to.

Ben phoned the hospital and arranged for Helen to be seen that afternoon then escorted her out. Emily laid fresh paper on the couch in readiness for her next patient, thinking about what had happened. So Ben had proved that he was a good doctor, a caring doctor—so what? It didn't alter the fact that he had treated her appallingly three years ago. Maybe he'd had his reasons for not believing her; she was willing to concede that. However, he had never even considered the idea that she may have been telling him the truth.

That's what hurt the most, the fact that he had been so sure that she'd been lying. It made her see that all those claims he'd made that meeting her was the best thing that had ever happened to him had been so much hot air. He'd been spinning her a line, telling her what she had wanted to hear to get her into bed. Not that she'd been exactly reluctant—definitely not! However, she had slept with him because she had been falling in love with him, whereas Ben had slept with her because she'd been convenient. Love hadn't entered the equation so far as he was concerned. And it wasn't part of the equation now.

Emily took a deep breath then summoned her next

patient. So long as she remembered that, everything would be fine.

Ben saw Helen out and went back to his room. He sat down, thinking about what had happened. Helen's grief had affected him deeply, mainly because it reinforced all his doubts about long-term relationships. He hated to think that any woman would have to go through that kind of heartache because of him. It also made him wonder if he was right to involve himself in Theo's life. If anything happened to him, he couldn't bear to think that his son would suffer.

It was something he needed to think about, he realised. He had acted instinctively when he'd found out about Theo; he hadn't stopped to consider the consequences. However, if he became an important part of Theo's life and the cancer did return, he could end up hurting him. On the other hand, if he didn't make every effort to get to know Theo, he would always regret it, especially if he remained fit and healthy.

He sighed. If only he could look into the future and see what it held, it would be so much easier, but that wasn't possible. It would help too if he could talk it through with Emily and find out what she thought, but he couldn't see that happening. Emily's only concern was Theo's welfare and he couldn't blame her for that. If he put doubts in her mind then she might very well refuse him access to the child. Until he was sure about what he was doing, he couldn't risk upsetting her. However, he would proceed with caution. Although he longed for the day when Theo called him daddy, he mustn't rush things. He had to take it slowly, accept that he might only ever be on the periphery of his son's life. Maybe it wasn't what he wanted but it was better than running the risk of Theo getting hurt.

The day came to an end and Emily was glad to be able to leave. She headed out to her car, wondering how she was going to get through the rest of the week. Being around Ben had been a strain. She was so aware of him that each time she'd needed to consult him, her heart had raced and she'd had problems breathing. Maybe he'd be here only for a matter of days but a lot could happen in that time, as she knew from experience. It had taken just one week, just *seven* days, for her to fall in love with him, after all. Her mouth compressed. She wasn't going to make that mistake again!

She left the surgery and drove across town. Her parents had collected Theo from nursery and taken him back to their house for tea. Although Emily knew how much Theo enjoyed spending time with his grandparents, she couldn't help wishing that she could have gone straight home. Her mother was far too astute and would soon realise that there was something worrying her.

What was she going to tell her? Emily wondered as she turned into the lane leading to Jackson's farm. She had never mentioned Ben to her parents but she would have to tell them about him soon. After all, if Tom had spotted the resemblance between him and Theo, other people would notice it too. It wasn't fair to keep her parents in the dark when everyone knew that Ben was Theo's father.

Emily had no idea how to set about it and racked

her brain as she drove along the lane. Now that hay-making was finished, the fields were being ploughed ready for planting and she slowed when she spotted her father driving one of the tractors. Maybe it would be easier if she told her dad first and enlisted his help to tell her mother?

Noel Jackson brought the tractor to a halt when Emily beeped her horn. He smiled as he watched her climb over the gate. 'Theo's helping your mum feed the chickens. They should be just about finished by now, I expect.'

'He loves feeding the chickens,' Emily agreed, pick-ing her way across the rough ground. She hesitated, wondering how to begin. Her parents had been so good about Theo. They had never tried to force her to tell them about his father and had done everything they could to help her. She only hoped they wouldn't be too disappointed in her when they found out their beloved grandson was the result of a brief affair.

'What's up, love? I can tell something's worrying you.'

'It's Theo,' Emily said when she heard the concern in her father's voice.

'There's nothing wrong with him, is there?' Noel said anxiously. 'He seemed right as rain to me.'

'No, no, he's fine,' she said hurriedly. She took a deep breath then rushed on before her courage deserted her. 'It's just that…well, his father has turned up.'

CHAPTER SIX

'Now you sit there and watch this new DVD that Granny has bought for you.' Emily got Theo settled on the sofa. 'I'll just be in the kitchen talking to Granny and Grandpa. Okay?'

She left Theo watching his film and went back to the kitchen. By tacit consent they hadn't discussed the issue uppermost on their minds during tea. Although her father had briefly told her mum about Ben turning up, they'd avoided speaking about him in front of Theo. Now she guessed that she would have a lot of questions to answer and sighed. She didn't want her parents to think too badly about Ben, oddly enough.

'Tea or coffee, darling?' Frances Jackson looked round when Emily entered the room. She smiled at her. 'Your dad and I are having tea but it's no trouble to make coffee if you'd prefer it.'

'Tea's fine, Mum. Thanks.' Emily sat down at the table and looked around. 'Where's Dad?'

'He thought it might be easier for you if he wasn't here,' Frances explained as she brought the pot over to the table. 'He's taken his tea through to the office to drink it there.'

'He didn't need to do that,' Emily protested. 'He has to know what happened at some point.'

'Of course. But I think he was worried in case he said the wrong thing.' Frances smiled ruefully. 'The idea of any man leaving his little girl in the lurch does tend to send him off at the deep end, I'm afraid.'

'I had no idea,' Emily admitted. 'I've caused you both an awful lot of heartache, haven't I?'

'Nonsense! On the contrary, you've given us the most wonderful gift we could ever have had—a gorgeous little grandson.' Frances patted her hand. 'I'll fill your dad in later, so don't you worry about that. From the sound of it, you've enough on your plate.'

Emily sighed. 'You're right. I never expected Ben to turn up like this.'

'So that's his name, is it—Ben?'

'Yes. Benedict Legrange. His father was French and his mother's English.'

'I see. And how did you meet him?' Frances asked quietly.

'He was staying with Simon and Ros while he recuperated from some sort of tropical disease he'd caught while working abroad,' Emily explained. 'He's a doctor—he worked with Tom at one point—and it was Tom who arranged it.'

'So this must have been soon after you returned to Bride's Bay,' Frances said, frowning.

'Yes, it was.'

'I always thought…' Frances broke off and shrugged. 'Well, it doesn't really matter now what I thought.'

'You thought Paul was Theo's father?' Emily shook

her head. 'No. Paul and I split up several months before I came back here.'

'I see. So what happened when you discovered you were pregnant? Did you tell Ben or what?'

'Oh, yes, I told him.' Emily smiled sadly. 'He'd returned to Paris by the time I realised I was expecting his child and I flew over there to see him.'

'How did he take it?' Frances asked, stirring her tea.

'Not very well.' Emily's voice caught. 'He accused me of lying, said that I was trying to pass off someone else's child as his.'

'What!' The spoon clattered into the saucer as Frances stared at her in consternation. 'He actually said that?'

'Yes. You can imagine how devastated I was.' Emily bit her lip when she felt tears well to her eyes. 'I couldn't believe he would accuse me of doing such a terrible thing.'

'Pity help him when your dad hears that!' Frances exploded.

Emily shook her head. All of a sudden she knew that she couldn't bear it if her parents took against Ben. 'No, you mustn't blame him. There was a reason why Ben thought I was lying, a reason I've only just found out about myself.'

'Really? It would have to be a very good reason, is all I can say.'

'It was. Apparently, he had cancer a few years ago and he was told that he would never be able to father a child because of the drugs he was given.'

'Well, I suppose that does make a difference,'

Frances conceded. 'But he didn't tell you all that when you went to see him?'

'No. I wish he had. I just thought that he didn't want anything more to do with me and that was why he accused me of lying—so he could get rid of me.'

'It must have been awful for you, darling. I wish you'd told me all this sooner. I feel terrible now because I had no idea what an ordeal you've been through.' Frances' voice was filled with remorse and Emily shook her head.

'You aren't to blame for any of it, Mum. If it weren't for you and Dad then I would never have managed as well as I have done.' She looked up when the back door opened as her father came in and smiled. 'You two have been brilliant. Nobody could have asked for better parents.'

'We just want you to be happy, don't we, Noel?' Frances said as her husband came to join them.

'That's right. Making sure that you and Theo are taken care of is our main concern.' His expression darkened. 'Now about Theo's father. I don't know what happened between you two—no doubt your mother will fill me in later. But if he's set on causing trouble then he'll have me to answer to. Nobody leaves my little girl in the lurch like he did and gets away with it!'

'Thanks, Dad, but it's a bit more complicated than that,' Emily replied then looked round when she heard Theo coming along the hall. They deliberately changed the subject as none of them wanted Theo to hear something he shouldn't. However, Emily knew it wasn't the end of the matter and that at some point her parents would want to meet Ben. Although she didn't relish the idea, she couldn't refuse after everything they had done for her. All she could hope was that her father wouldn't do anything rash. Maybe *she* hadn't forgiven Ben for the way he had treated her, but it didn't mean she wanted him to be at odds with her family, strangely enough.

She took Theo home a short time later. Her parents waved them off, standing side by side outside the farmhouse. Emily couldn't help envying them their closeness. They had the sort of loving and supportive relationship she had always dreamt of, the kind of relationship she had once hoped she would have with Ben, although not any longer. He might be Theo's father but that was all he would ever be. Even if she did allow him access to Theo, it wouldn't change things. They may be Theo's parents but they would never be a proper family. Her heart ached at the thought even though she knew how foolish it was to let it upset her.

Ben couldn't settle. Although he tried to join in the conversation as they sat around the table after dinner, drinking coffee, he was too distracted. He kept thinking about Emily, thinking about how hurt she must have been when he had accused her of lying. No wonder she didn't want anything to do with him!

'You're going to have to sort this out or you'll drive yourself mad.'

Tom's voice cut into his thoughts and Ben looked up. 'I beg your pardon?'

'This situation with Emily. You need to sort it out.' Tom shook his head when Ben automatically started to protest. 'Don't bother. There's no point claiming that you aren't thinking about her when it's as plain as the nose on your face that you are.'

Ben sighed. 'I just wish that I'd behaved differently when she came to see me.'

'I can understand that but there's no point dwelling on it. It's what you're going to do now that matters,' Tom said encouragingly. 'How you're going to make things right between you.'

'I'm starting to think that's an impossibility.' He shrugged when his friend raised his brows. 'Emily has made it clear that she's not exactly my biggest fan.'

'So change her mind, prove that you're sorry for what you did and that you only have her and Theo's best interests at heart.' Tom paused and looked at him. 'You do, I assume?'

'Of course!' Ben declared forcefully.

'Good.' Tom grinned at him. 'So what's stopping you from driving over to Emily's house this very minute and telling her how you feel? There's no time like the present, or so they say.'

'Stop bullying poor Ben,' Hannah protested. She smiled at Ben. 'Although I have to say that I agree with Tom. The sooner you get this sorted, the better for everyone, and especially Theo. He's such a lovely little boy and he'll love having his daddy around. It's the best thing that could have happened to him.'

Ben just smiled, not wanting to explain that he had doubts about that. He still hadn't made up his mind if he was doing the right thing by getting involved in Theo's life when there was no guarantee that he'd be around while the child grew up. However, until he had thought it all through properly he would keep his concerns to himself. Even though he didn't intend to rush things, he still wanted to get to know Theo. In fact, he couldn't wait to see him again. And Emily too, although he refused to delve too deeply into the reason why when she'd done everything possible to discourage him.

He stood up, unable to sit there any longer, torturing himself. He needed to take some sort of action even if he did decide in the end that it would be better for Theo if he didn't get too close to him. 'You've convinced me. I shall go to see Emily and hope that we can work things out.'

'It might be better if you phoned first,' Hannah suggested hurriedly, but he shrugged.

'What is the point? She will only tell me that she's too busy to see me.' He laughed thinly, hoping his friends couldn't hear the hurt in his voice. Even though he knew he shouldn't let Emily's attitude affect him, it did. 'I'm very much persona non grata where Emily is concerned.'

Hannah didn't say anything but Ben could tell she wasn't convinced he was doing the right thing by turning up unannounced. As he fetched his car keys, he realised that he had no idea how Emily would react. She would either let him in or, as seemed more likely, send him on his way, but it was worth a try. There were just four days left before he went back to Paris and he needed every second to press home his case.

He drove to Emily's cottage, working out what he would say when he saw her. However, there was no sign of her car when he arrived. She'd obviously gone out so he parked outside her neighbour's house and switched off the engine while he waited. She would have to return at some point, of course. She would need to put Theo to bed, so she couldn't stay out all night…

Unless she had no intention of returning.

Ben's heart turned over. Surely she wouldn't just up and leave to escape him, would she? He tried to convince himself that it was crazy to harbour such a notion, but he only had to recall how she'd behaved around him that day to know that it was possible. He swore under his breath. If he had driven Emily away then he would never forgive himself!

Theo was fast asleep by the time Emily turned into the lane leading to the cottage. He was normally in bed way before now so it wasn't surprising. She rounded the bend, mentally crossing her fingers that she would be able to get him into bed without waking him. She really couldn't face the thought of a lot of hassle to-night of all nights.

She parked on the drive and got out. Hunting her key out of her bag, she went to unlock the front door then jumped when a figure suddenly materialised out of the gloom. It was a moment before she recognised Ben and she glared at him.

'You scared the life out of me! What on earth do you think you're doing, lurking in the shadows?'

'I'm sorry. I didn't mean to frighten you.' He stepped forward and she could see genuine concern on his face. 'Are you all right?'

'Yes,' Emily snapped because she didn't appreciate the fact that her heart was hammering in the most ridiculous fashion. She opened the door then turned to him. 'I don't know what you want, Ben, and frankly I don't care. I need to put Theo to bed so whatever it is will have to wait.'

'Fine. I'm more than happy to wait.' He glanced towards the car. 'Shall I fetch Theo in for you?'

'No!' Emily rounded on him. Although she wasn't sure if he was being deliberately obtuse, she wasn't prepared to give him the benefit of the doubt. 'I have nothing to say to you tonight or any other night. Is that clear?'

'Perfectly. However, willing me to disappear isn't going to work, I'm afraid. We need to talk and we need to do so soon.'

He shrugged, his broad shoulders moving lightly under the thin navy cotton sweater he was wearing, and Emily felt a surge of heat race along her veins and looked away. She hated being so aware of him. She should be immune to him after the way he had treated her, but there was no point pretending that she was. Ben only had to look at her and her knees went weak. He only had to smile and her heart raced. It had been the same three years ago and little had changed if today was anything to go by. She wanted him now just as much as she had wanted him then and the fact that she was so weak filled her with self-loathing. Her mind might know that Ben was bad news, but her body didn't. All her body could think about was how it had felt to lie in his arms and love him, to have him love her in return...

She turned away, uncaring what he thought as she pushed past him and lifted a sleepy Theo out of the car. She carried him inside and up the stairs, ignoring Ben as he followed in her wake. Pushing open the door to Theo's bedroom, she gently laid him on the rug and stripped off his shorts. Although he was dry during the day, he still needed a nappy at night so she popped it on then wiped his hands and face with a damp flannel and put on the bottom half of his favourite dinosaur pyjamas. Scooping him up, she laid him in his cot-bed and covered him with a light cotton blanket.

'Night, night, sleep tight,' she whispered, stroking his shiny dark curls. 'Mind the bugs don't…'

'Bite,' he murmured sleepily, closing his eyes.

Turning, she left the room, leaving Ben to do as he pleased. He could stay there and watch Theo or he could follow her downstairs; she really didn't care. Walking into the sitting room, she switched on the lamp, her whole body trembling as reaction set in. Today had been an ordeal and it wasn't over yet. Ben was going to have his say whether she wanted him to or not, so maybe it would be simpler if they got it over with. It didn't mean she was going to allow him to walk all over her, however. Maybe she *had* defended him to her parents but she hadn't forgiven him and couldn't imagine doing so either.

Could she?

Emily took a quick breath as she heard footsteps coming down the stairs. She had always believed that she would never forgive Ben for the way he had treated her but that had been before she'd found out why he had been so cruel. Although it still hurt to know that he had believed her capable of such deceit, it had made a difference. That was why she'd been at pains to explain his actions to her parents, she realised. She'd wanted to be fair, to tell them his side of the story, not just hers. Maybe he hadn't loved her, but she couldn't punish him for that. He'd had his reasons for not believing her, good reasons, too, and she had to accept that and not allow the hurt she felt to stop her doing what was right for Theo. And if that meant allowing Ben to play a role in Theo's life then she would have to consider it.

It all sounded so logical in theory. However, as Ben came into the room, Emily knew it wasn't going to be straightforward. When she looked at him she didn't simply see the father of her child but the man she had once loved with all her heart. There was no denying that she still had feelings for him, either, if today was anything to go by, and that would further complicate matters. She needed to keep a clear head, weigh up the situation and make sure she did what was best for Theo. Theo was the important one. How *she* felt was irrelevant. She couldn't allow her emotions to get in the way when she made any decisions.

Emily bit her lip as a rush of panic assailed her. There wasn't a doubt in her mind that being around Ben was going to test her control to the absolute limit!

CHAPTER SEVEN

'THEO's fast asleep,' Ben said quietly as he came into the room. He sat down, wishing that Emily would say something. She was staring at him with the strangest expression on her face…

She stood up abruptly. 'Do you want a cup of coffee?'

'If you're having one,' he replied politely.

'I am.'

She left the room and Ben frowned. What had he seen on her face just now? he wondered. It had been such an odd mixture of emotions yet for a moment he'd thought he had seen real awareness in her eyes…

He stood up abruptly and went over to the window, knowing how stupid it was to let that idea take hold. Emily wasn't interested in him *that* way; she wasn't interested in him any way! He knew it was true yet as he stared at the darkening view, he could feel his body quickening in a way that was all too familiar. Three years ago, he'd only had to look at her to feel his desire rising and it was happening again, right here, right now, this very minute. He wanted her, so help him, wanted to take her in his arms and taste the sweetness of her lips, feel the soft curves of her body under his…

He groaned, feeling the blood pounding through his veins as he went and sat down. It had been years since he'd felt this way, so hungry, so filled with need. Resting his head against the cushions, he tried to remember when he'd last experienced this kind of all-consuming desire and felt his stomach sink when he realised that it had been the last time he'd made love to Emily. Oh, there'd been women since then, of course, not very many but a few; however, he had never felt like this with them. If he was being completely honest, he had never felt this way with anyone except Emily.

'Here you are.'

Ben jumped when a hand appeared in front of him holding a cup of coffee. He straightened up, cursing his own weakness. He'd come here with the express intention of convincing Emily to allow him to see Theo, not to try to get her back into his bed!

'Merci.' He took a sip of the coffee and winced when he discovered how strong it was. He put the cup down, wondering if she'd deliberately made it that way. Emily knew he loathed strong coffee, so had it been an act of defiance, a less than subtle hint that she had no intention of pandering to him? He couldn't say for sure but, if recent events were anything to go by, it seemed likely.

The thought wasn't reassuring but he refused to let it deter him. He waited until she had sat down then leant forward. 'The first thing I want to make clear is that I do not wish to cause any trouble.'

'Really? You do surprise me.' She took a sip of coffee, watching him over the rim of the cup with cold green eyes, and Ben swallowed his sigh. She wasn't prepared to give an inch, which made his task all the harder.

'I only want what's best for you and Theo, Emily.'

She laughed out loud. 'Oh, please! Do you honestly think I'm going to fall for that old chestnut?'

'It's the truth. Whether you choose to believe it is up to you, but I want to do what's right, what I feel is right in here.' He touched his chest. 'For both of you.'

'Very commendable, I'm sure. What a pity you didn't feel like that three years ago.'

Ben heard her voice catch and hated himself all over again for having caused her so much pain. 'I know that nothing I do can ever make up for what I said to you that day, but it will be different in the future, Emily. I promise you that.'

'I don't care about me. I've had three years to get over it. It's Theo I'm worried about. I don't want him getting hurt.'

'And I shall never hurt him.' Ben took a deep breath, doing his best to rein in the doubts that had surfaced again. No matter what happened, he needed to get to know his son, even if their relationship might never be as close as he hoped it would. 'I swear on my life that I shall never do anything to hurt Theo. I just want the chance to get to know him. That's all I'm asking for, Emily—to spend some time with him.'

'It might be all for now but who's to say that things won't change in the future?' She looked him in the eyes. 'What happens if you decide that you want to be more than a part-time father, Ben? After all, if you can't father another child, you may decide that you want Theo.'

'No! I shall never try to take Theo away from you, if that's what you fear. Even if I never have another child—and I honestly can't see it happening—I would never do that to you, Emily.'

'That's not what you said the other day. You told me that you'd do anything it took to get access to Theo.' She shrugged. 'It's a small step from gaining access to going for custody.'

'I was angry and upset, and I said things I shouldn't have said.' Ben ran his hand through his hair, wishing that he'd handled the situation better. Right from the outset his behaviour had left much to be desired. 'Theo's your son, Emily, and he needs you far more than he needs me.' His voice caught as all his fears surfaced. 'You'll be here for him for as long as he needs you. I can't promise to do that, even though I wish with all my heart that I could.'

Emily had no idea what Ben meant. Why couldn't he promise to stay around? Was there something he wasn't telling her? Her mind raced this way and that and finally alighted on an explanation, one she found so unpalatable that it was a moment before she could speak.

'You mean that your current girlfriend might not approve of you spending time with your love child?'

She laughed harshly, wondering why she had never thought about Ben being involved with someone else. After all, it was unlikely that he'd been celibate for the past three years; there must have been many women during that time. Maybe one of them had done what she'd been unable to do and made him fall in love with her?

The thought was way too painful and she shot to her feet. 'It would be best if you spoke to her and found out how she felt. There seems little point in you upsetting Theo's life if she isn't prepared to accept him.'

'You've got it all wrong!' He stood up as well, his dark eyes blazing as he took a step towards her. 'I don't have a girlfriend or anyone else whom I need to consult.' Reaching out he caught hold of her shoulders, holding her still when she tried to turn away. 'This is about us, Emily, you, me and Theo, nobody else.'

Emily felt her head swirl. Maybe it was the result of all the tension she'd been under that day, but all of a sudden she felt a wave of dizziness engulf her. Ben must have realised something was wrong because he put his arm around her.

'Are you all right?' he asked, bending to look into her face.

'I'm fine,' she replied, although it was a lie. The room seemed to be whirling around and she closed her eyes.

'You're not fine at all,' he said firmly, drawing her to him so that her head was cushioned against his shoulder.

Emily longed to push him away but she was afraid that she would fall over if she did so. She could feel the heat from his body seeping into hers, chasing away the chill that had invaded her, and tears rose to her eyes. She didn't want to feel this way, didn't want to feel *anything* for him!

'Shh, don't upset yourself, *chérie*. You will feel better in a moment.'

His tone was so gentle, so caring, that Emily cried all the harder, deep racking sobs that seemed to spring from some dark and lonely place inside her. After she had returned from seeing Ben in Paris, she hadn't allowed herself to cry. Keeping control of her emotions had been important both for her own state of mind as well as for her baby's. Once Theo was born it had seemed even more vital to maintain her composure. She didn't want Theo growing up with a mother who was constantly moping around. Now it was as though all the pent-up emotions had come flooding out and she couldn't stop them.

When Ben led her over to the sofa, she didn't resist. He sat down and drew her into his arms, stroking her hair while he murmured to her in French. Even though she couldn't understand what he was saying, she drew comfort from the tone of his voice so that gradually her sobs lessened. He put his hand under her chin, tilting her face up so that he could look at her and his eyes were filled with a concern that warmed her.

'I hate to see you crying like that, *chérie*, even though I suspect it may have done you good.' He brushed her wet cheeks with his thumbs, wiping away the last glistening tears, and she shivered.

'I…I try not to get upset for Theo's sake,' she whispered, lowering her eyes in case he saw something he shouldn't. She didn't want Ben to know that she still had feelings for him; it would only complicate matters.

'You've been very brave for a long time,' he murmured, his deep voice rumbling softly. He tipped her chin up again. 'I wish that I had been here for you, Emily. I wish that I had been here for Theo, too. It's something I shall regret until the day I die.'

His voice caught and she felt shock run through her when she saw tears in his eyes this time. She reacted instinctively, putting her arms around his neck as she drew his head down onto her shoulder. There wasn't a doubt in her mind that what he was feeling was very real and all of a sudden the hurt and anger she'd felt these past years faded into nothing. Ben was hurting and she wanted to comfort him as he had comforted her.

'It's all right. I understand now why you said what you did. I only wish you'd told me sooner…about the cancer and your treatment.'

'I wish I had too. But I was so hurt…so angry.' He broke off, rubbing his hand over his eyes, and she could tell that he was embarrassed about losing control. Ben was a very private person who guarded his emotions probably because he had learned to do so. Getting through an ordeal like he'd been through took tremendous strength of mind and he had learned to keep his feelings locked away.

It was a light bulb moment, a glimpse behind the handsome exterior to the man inside, and Emily knew that it had made a world of difference to the way she thought about him. However, now wasn't the time to dwell on it. She sighed softly. 'It must have been a shock for you when I turned up and announced that I was expecting your child.'

'It was.' He captured her hand and raised it to his lips, pressing a kiss to her palm in a gesture that brought back far too many memories. 'I'd been told that the odds against me fathering a child were several billion to one. I'd seen the test results as well and they'd appeared conclusive. That's why I couldn't accept what you were telling me.'

'I can understand that now.' Emily drew her hand away, not wanting to start something she would regret. It would be far too easy to allow the emotions that were swirling around them to take over, but it would be wrong. They needed to talk this through, see if they could find some common ground for Theo's sake. 'However, there's no point dwelling on the past. We need to decide what we're going to do about Theo.'

'And you think we can do that? You think we can reach some sort of…understanding?'

There was something in his voice which made her tremble inside but she refused to acknowledge it. Ben was talking about their son; anything else was the product of her overactive imagination. 'I don't see why not. After all, we both want the same thing, don't we? We want what's best for Theo so that will make it easier, surely?'

'Yes. I want what's best for Theo but not if it means upsetting you, Emily.' His tone was level. There was no hint of anything in it, nothing to make her wonder if he wanted to reach an understanding with her too.

Emily swallowed her disappointment, knowing how foolish it was to imagine he cared about her. 'There's no reason why I should get upset, Ben. You've told me that you have no wish to take Theo away from me so I don't see why we can't reach an agreement about access. Obviously, it isn't going to be easy, with you living in Paris, but it isn't impossible.' She shrugged. 'I can bring Theo over to see you or you can come here.'

'You'd do that? You would bring Theo to Paris to visit me?'

'Of course. Obviously I won't be able to do it every week…'

'Of course not!' He laughed, his voice filled with such happiness that she found herself laughing as well.

'Hmm, I do have a tendency to state the obvious, don't I? Sorry!'

'You have nothing to apologise for, Emily. Nothing at all.'

He smiled into her eyes and this time there was no mistaking what she could see in his. Emily felt her breath catch when she saw the desire in them. Ben wanted her; she could tell that from the way he was looking at her. It was hard to focus when her heart was racing.

'You've given me something I never dreamt I would have, Emily, and I shall always be grateful to you for that.' He brushed his knuckles across her cheek. 'You're the mother of my child and I can't tell you how much that means to me.'

There was a moment when Emily knew that she should stop what was happening, yet she let it pass. When Ben bent and touched his mouth to hers, she didn't protest. Maybe it was madness but all of a sudden she wanted his kiss and there was no point pretending otherwise. He slowly drew back and his very reluctance warmed her. Ben might not love her as she'd once hoped, but he felt something for her.

'Thank you. Thank you from the bottom of my heart for everything, Emily.'

'Thank you too.'

He frowned. 'What for?'

She laughed softly, not wanting him to suspect how much it meant to her to discover that he wasn't indifferent to her, after all. 'Without you, I wouldn't have Theo. I can't imagine how empty my life would be without him.'

Ben's face broke into a smile. 'Theo is a lucky little boy to have you for his mother.' He gave her a hug then stood up. 'I'd better go. You have to be up early in the morning for work.'

'We both do.'

Emily stood up too, clamping down on the thought of how much she would have liked him to stay. It would be foolish to go down that route. She should be content with what they had achieved, which was far more than she had expected. At least when Ben returned to Paris at the end of the week, they should have sorted this out.

The thought spurred her on as she saw him to the door. She paused with her hand on the latch. 'Would you like to come for supper tomorrow? I finish early on Wednesdays so I'll have more time to cook. You can play with Theo while I get the meal ready.'

'I'd love to!' he exclaimed in delight. 'Thank you for asking me.'

'It's no trouble.' She opened the door, stepping aside so he could pass her. He paused and she could see the tenderness in his eyes.

'Until tomorrow, *chérie*.' Bending, he brushed her cheek with a kiss then left.

Emily watched him get into his car and even managed to wave as he drove away but her heart was hammering. She went back inside and sat down while she thought about what had happened, but her mind kept skipping over the details and coming back to those kisses. She shivered. A couple of kisses didn't mean anything and she would be a fool to imagine that they did. Ben had kissed her because he'd wanted to apologise. He'd kissed her because he'd been grateful. He had kissed her for all sorts of reasons apart from one. Ben didn't love her and she mustn't make the mistake of thinking that he did.

CHAPTER EIGHT

BEN was on a high the following day. Knowing that he would be seeing Emily and Theo that night made the time fly. He got through his morning and evening lists without any hitches, deriving a great deal of satisfaction from solving his patients' problems.

As he took the files through to the office after he'd finished, he realised how low he had been feeling recently. Although it had been hard work setting up the clinic, it wasn't the pressure of work that had been affecting him but this situation with Emily. Ever since Tom had mentioned her, he had felt on edge. Even though he had tried not to think about that period in his life, he had never managed to erase it. It had been like a wound that wouldn't heal but now he knew the truth, it was very different. Emily hadn't lied to him. She hadn't tried to use him. Knowing that made him feel so much better.

'Ah, Ben, there you are. How did you get on? Not too stressful a day, I hope?'

Ben smiled when the head of the practice, Simon Harper, came into the office. 'Not at all. In fact, I'd go so far as to say that I enjoyed it.'

'Really?' Simon laughed. 'Well, that makes me feel much better. I have to confess that I was starting to feel a bit guilty about accepting your help when you're supposed to be here on holiday.'

'There's no need,' Ben assured him. 'I've been so tied up with paperwork lately that it makes a welcome change to do some hands-on medicine for once.'

'I can imagine how hard it must have been for you after your father died,' Simon sympathised.

'It was.' Ben sighed. 'Setting up the clinic was my father's dream and that made it all the harder.'

'Because you wanted to do things the way he would have wanted them done,' Simon suggested astutely.

'Yes, although I've come to realise that it isn't always possible.' He shrugged. 'I've had to make several changes to his plans but I think he would have approved.'

'I'm sure he would.' Simon clapped him on the shoulder. 'He would have been proud of you, Ben. There's nothing like seeing your children come into their own, as I'm sure you'll discover for yourself one day.'

It was the sort of throwaway comment that would have made very little impact at one time. However, as Ben left the office, it struck him how different it was now that he had a child of his own. He could imagine how proud he would be of Theo as he watched him growing up... If he got the chance. Once again the doubts reared their ugly heads but he stamped them down. He refused to allow anything to spoil the evening. This was his first real chance to get to know his son and he wouldn't let anything take the shine off it.

He drove straight to Emily's, briefly stopping en route to buy some flowers for her and a gift for Theo. Although he didn't intend to turn into the sort of father who bribed his child with presents at every turn, he couldn't bear to turn up empty-handed. After all, he had missed two birthdays and two Christmases so surely Emily would make allowances?

He parked outside then walked up the path and knocked on the door. Emily opened it, smiling as she invited him inside.

'Come on in. Supper won't be long. I'm just waiting for the potatoes to finish baking.'

'These are for you.' Ben handed her the flowers.

'Oh, you shouldn't have!' she exclaimed but he could tell that she was pleased by his gift.

He smiled at her, loving the hint of colour that had bloomed in her cheeks. It was good to know that he'd had a positive effect on her for once. 'Of course I should. I'm just pleased you like them.'

'I do. Thank you.'

She gave him a quick smile then led the way to the sitting room where Theo was playing with some building blocks. Ben paused in the doorway, feeling a whole host of emotions well up inside him. This was his son, the child he had never thought he would have; he couldn't begin to explain how it made him feel.

'Theo, this is Ben. He came to see us the other day if you remember. Come and say hello, darling.'

Emily urged the little boy to his feet, holding his hand as she led him across the room. Ben crouched down, guessing it would be less intimidating for Theo if they were on the same eye level.

'Hello, Theo. It's nice to see you again,' he said softly. He held out the package he'd brought. 'This is for you.'

Theo stared at the parcel for a moment then slowly reached out and took it off him. Kneeling down, he stripped off the paper, exclaiming in delight when he saw the bright red car that Ben had bought for him. Within moments, he had the box open and was busily running it across the floor.

Emily laughed. 'You couldn't have bought him anything better. He *adores* cars.'

'Good. I'll make a note of that,' Ben said lightly, trying not to let her see how moved he was by his first proper encounter with his son.

'You do that. Right, I'll leave you two to enjoy yourselves while I carry on getting the supper ready,' Emily told him with a gentle smile, and Ben swallowed his sigh. He could tell that she understood how he felt but then nobody had ever been able to read him as well as Emily could.

It was something he knew he needed to bear in mind. He couldn't afford to do anything that might upset her. He had to concentrate on being a good father to Theo because that was all Emily wanted him to be, her son's father, not her lover. Would he be able to handle the change in their relationship? he wondered. In the past three years he had convinced himself that he was over her, that any feelings he'd had for her were dead. It had been easier that way, less painful. However, as he watched her leave the room, he felt his heart lurch. Knowing that Emily hadn't tried to use him had changed everything. He was no longer sure how he felt, if he was honest.

'More carrots, Ben?'

Emily passed the vegetable dish across the table. On the surface the evening had gone smoothly. Theo seemed to have accepted Ben's presence, which was encouraging. Although Theo could be shy around strangers, he seemed to have taken to Ben readily enough. She knew she should be pleased that things were working out so well and she was. It was just that she sensed a certain tension that unsettled her. It made her wonder if there was something Ben wasn't telling her.

She brushed aside that thought as she helped Theo spoon up the last of his peas. There was no point looking for trouble that might not exist. 'That's a good boy. Would you like a yoghurt now?'

When Theo nodded, she went to the fridge and took out a pot of his favourite raspberry dessert. She placed it in front of him then glanced at Ben, feeling the colour run up her cheeks when she discovered that he was watching her. 'I'm afraid I haven't made a pudding for us. There's cheese or fruit though if you'd like some.'

'Nothing for me, thank you. That chicken was delicious and so were the vegetables. I haven't tasted any as fresh for ages.'

'We have my mother to thank for them. Mum keeps me well stocked with fruit and veg,' she explained, switching on the kettle to make coffee. Just because Ben had been watching her, it didn't mean anything.

'She's a keen gardener, I take it?'

'You could say that.' Emily laughed, glad of the distraction. She had to stop being so aware of Ben and treat him like everyone else. 'She takes first prize for her vegetables at the county show most years. Nobody else gets a look-in!'

'It must be rather disheartening for them,' he said with a smile.

'I'm sure it is.'

'Your parents have a farm, don't they?'

'That's right. It's mainly dairy, although they've had to diversify in the past few years and not just rely on the milk yield. They make their own cheeses now and have started to produce yoghurt as well. That's one of theirs that Theo is eating, in fact.'

'A lot of farmers in France have had to branch out. More and more have set up their own businesses to boost their income.'

'It was the same for Mum and Dad. The supermarkets have squeezed every penny of profit out of milk production. Dad was starting to wonder if he'd have to give up farming when Mum persuaded him to let her try her hand at making cheese.' She shrugged. 'Fortunately, it took off almost immediately and now that side of the business generates the most profit.'

'It would have been awful if they'd had to leave the farm,' Ben said sympathetically.

'It would. There's been Jacksons farming in this area for the past six generations.'

'Do you think Theo will continue the trend?'

Emily laughed. 'It's a bit early to say although I have to admit that he adores helping out around the farm. Feeding the chickens is one of his favourite things. It's definitely a close second to playing with his cars!'

Ben laughed as well, his handsome face lighting up in a way that made her breath catch. Emily turned away, busying herself with making their coffee. Ben was Theo's father and that was all, she reminded herself as she carried the pot over to the table. That he was a very attractive man was neither here nor there. Theo had finished his yoghurt so she wiped his mouth and lifted him down from the table.

'Go and play with your new car, darling, while Ben and I drink our coffee. We won't be long.'

Ben smiled as he watched the little boy hurry out of the room. 'He's no trouble, is he?'

'Oh, he has his moments, believe me,' Emily warned him, pouring coffee for them both. She passed the sugar bowl across the table then sat down. Ben spooned some sugar into his cup then glanced up.

'It can't have been easy for you, Emily. Looking after a child and working is a lot to cope with.'

'My parents helped. I couldn't have managed if they hadn't been so supportive, especially in the beginning.'

Ben's expression darkened. 'It should have been me helping you.'

'I thought we agreed that it was pointless dwelling on the past.' She sighed when he shook his head. 'I managed, Ben, so please stop beating yourself up because you weren't around.'

'I suppose you're right,' he conceded. 'But it still doesn't make me feel good to know what a hard time you must have had.'

'Forget it. It's what happens from now on that matters,' she told him, realising with a start that it was true. It was as though all the hurt and anger had disappeared and all she could think about now was how to make things right for Theo and Ben. She'd had such a happy childhood herself and she wanted the same for her son. She was convinced that Theo would only benefit from having both his mother and his father around while he was growing up.

'Obviously, I want to get to know Theo,' Ben said slowly.

Emily frowned when she heard the note of caution in his voice. Surely he wasn't having second thoughts, was he? 'But?' she challenged him. 'I get the distinct impression there was a but tagged onto the end of that statement.'

'Not really.' He shrugged. 'I just don't want Theo to get hurt.'

'There's no reason why he should. After all, as far as Theo is concerned you're just a friend of mine.'

'So you don't plan on telling him that I'm his father?'

'Not yet—no. He's only just met you, Ben. He would find it too confusing if I tried to explain that you're his daddy.'

'I see. Well, obviously, I'll be guided by you. You know him far better than I do.'

She'd expected him to protest and frowned when he accepted her decision without question. Once again the thought that he was holding back rose to her mind and she knew that she had to find out if she was right. If Ben wasn't committed to making this work then she wasn't prepared to risk upsetting Theo simply to satisfy a whim.

'You are sure this is what you want? If you aren't, Ben, then I'd prefer it if you told me now rather than let the situation progress any further.'

Ben took a deep breath. He knew that if he admitted he had doubts it could alter everything. However, if he didn't tell her, he would be guilty of lying by default and he couldn't bear to do that, to mislead her after everything else that had happened. 'Yes, it's what I want. I want to be a proper father to Theo more than anything. However, it may not be possible.'

'I don't understand.' She looked at him in confusion. 'If you're as committed to making this work as you claim then what's the problem?'

'The problem is that I have no idea how long I'm going to be around.' He sighed when she looked blankly at him. It wasn't easy to put his fears into words but now that he'd got this far, he had to explain. 'What if the cancer comes back, Emily? What if it can't be treated next time? How would it affect Theo if I died?'

A **treat** from us to **thank you** for reading our books!

Turn over **now** to find out more

Thanks for reading!

We're treating you to **TWO** fabulous offers...

2 FREE BOOKS

from your favourite Mills & Boon series plus have books delivered to your door every month!

Find out more and claim your free books at
www.millsandboon.co.uk/bookclub

or call 020 8288 2888 and
quote BOOKCLUB today!

Plus

15% OFF **

Your next order online with code
THANKSFEB at **www.millsandboon.co.uk**

MILLS &
BOON

CHAPTER NINE

BEN could feel his heart pounding. Thump, thump, thump, it went, as though someone was banging a drum. Emily was just sitting there as though frozen with shock and he wished with all his heart that he hadn't told her about his concerns, but how could he not have done so? She deserved to know the truth and if it meant that she changed her mind about letting him get to know Theo, he would have to accept it.

'I never thought…' She stopped and his stomach knotted in agony for causing her even more distress. She had been through enough thanks to him without him making her life even more complicated.

He stood up abruptly, knowing that he had to do the honourable thing. It had been wrong to think he could step into Theo's life, wrong and selfish. It was obvious from what he had seen that Theo was a happy and contented child, and why shouldn't he be? He had everything he could possibly need—a mother who adored him plus other family members who loved and cared about him. He didn't need a father, or at least he didn't need one who might end up letting him down!

'I'm sorry, Emily, I should never have started this.

It's obvious that Theo doesn't need me in his life, especially when I could end up hurting him.' He pushed his chair under the table. 'Obviously, I'll make arrangements to contribute towards his upkeep…'

'I don't want your money, Ben!'

She shot to her feet, her eyes blazing, and his stomach sank that bit more. He was trying his hardest not to make matters worse, but even his best efforts weren't good enough, he feared.

'It's only fair that I pay towards the cost of raising him,' he said flatly, trying not to let his emotions get in the way, not an easy task when he seemed to be awash with them. He didn't want to do this, couldn't bear to imagine how empty his life was going to be without Emily and Theo. It may only have been a few days since he'd realised that Theo was his son but even in that short time the child had become vitally important to him…as important as Emily was, in fact.

'Fair? What's fair about you running out on him? What's fair about you refusing to be a real father to him?' She rounded the table and glared at him. 'Theo doesn't need your money any more than I do. We manage extremely well, thank you very much.'

'In that case, I shall arrange some sort of trust fund for when he's older.' Even though he would have dearly loved to argue the point, Ben couldn't. His head was already reeling as he tried to deal with the thought of how important Emily was to him. Cutting himself off from her would be as big a wrench as cutting himself off from Theo.

'Fine. You do that. But don't be surprised if Theo

tells you thanks, but no thanks.' Her anger seemed to have increased, if anything. 'I doubt he'll be your number one fan after I tell him that you were too *scared* to be a proper father to him.'

Ben felt frustration pour through his veins. Why wouldn't she accept that it was the only thing he could do? Why did she have to make it even more difficult? 'I am not doing this because I'm scared.'

'No?'

The scorn in her voice whipped at nerves which were already raw and he glared at her. 'No. I'm doing this because it's the right thing to do, the sensible thing.'

'Oh, really?' She laughed harshly. 'Your idea of what makes sense is very different from mine, is all I can say. How sensible is it to change your mind about getting to know Theo because you're suddenly having cold feet?'

'It's rather more than a case of cold feet, Emily, as you very well know.' His tone was icy now, but it didn't cool her anger.

'I disagree. If you really wanted to be a proper father to Theo then you wouldn't allow anything to deter you. You're using your illness as a cop-out, Ben, and that's the truth.'

'I'm not familiar with the term, although I can guess what it means.' He stared coldly back at her, relieved to be in control once more. 'I will not be responsible for hurting Theo. That's what it all comes down to, Emily, whether you choose to believe me or not.'

'Which I don't.' She turned away but not before he'd seen the tears in her eyes, and his hard-won control shattered once more.

'I don't want to fight with you. It's the last thing I want.'

'Then change your mind.' She swung round. 'Don't cut yourself off like this, Ben. It isn't right, not for you or for Theo or…or for me.'

'I can't see how it will make any difference to you, Emily. In fact, I imagine it will make your life a lot simpler if I leave.'

'That's where you're wrong. Despite what you think, Theo needs a father. He needs you, Ben.' Her voice caught. 'I need you too.'

'You do?' Ben could feel it starting again, feel that crazy drumbeat pounding inside his chest. He took a step towards her then stopped, afraid that he would do something stupid if he got too close.

'Yes.' She bit her lip then continued in a rush. 'Oh, I know I've spent the last three years hating your guts, but now I know the truth about why you behaved the way you did, everything has changed. I want you to stay here and help me raise our son.'

'Because it's too big a task to do it all by yourself?' he suggested roughly, unconsciously taking another step.

'No. Because Theo needs both of us.' She looked up and the pounding seemed to reach a crescendo when he saw the expression on her face. Not even in his wildest dreams had he expected to see Emily look at him again with such longing in her eyes. 'And because I need you too.'

The words were barely out of her mouth before she was in his arms. Ben crushed her against him and it felt like a homecoming. When he held her in his arms, he felt safe, safe and in control of his life, which was the craziest thought of all bearing in mind that every cell in his body was running riot.

'Emily, I...' He started to speak and stopped. All of a sudden words weren't enough, certainly not enough to explain how he felt. Bending, he pressed his mouth to hers and let his lips tell her exactly what he wanted her to hear. Every nuance was there in the kiss, every syllable that couldn't be uttered. He hadn't understood how deeply he'd felt until that moment and it was a revelation to realise that he still wanted her, still ached for her; that he still loved her.

She drew back and he could see the confusion on her face and understood. He had never told her how he'd felt three years ago. Hell, he hadn't even admitted to himself that he had loved her! Living in the shadow of cancer had made him deny his feelings; he'd been too afraid of the consequences to face the truth. Now he could no longer hold back. He loved her and he always would. Maybe it was discovering that he had a child that had unlocked his emotions—he wasn't sure. But he could no longer pretend even if it was a shock for her. After all, Emily had spent the last three years hating him. To suddenly discover that he loved her must be hard to accept. Tenderness welled up inside him as he kissed her softly on the mouth.

'I'm sorry, Emily. I know this must be a shock for you.'

'It is. I never expected...' She stopped and he knew that she was afraid to say out loud what was in her head.

'That I loved you?' He kissed her again and smiled. 'If it's any consolation, it was a shock for me too. I had no idea how I really felt until a few seconds ago.'

'Didn't you?' she whispered.

'No. I honestly thought I was over you, that any feelings I'd had for you had died, but I was wrong.' He held her face between his hands. 'I love you, Emily. I know I shouldn't tell you that after everything I've done, but it's true. I love you.'

'I love you too.' She took a quick breath and he saw the dawning understanding on her face. 'I love you, Ben. I didn't think I did but I do!'

Reaching up, she kissed him and he felt her tremble. His arms tightened around her because he understood how overwhelmed she felt. He'd spent the last three years denying his feelings too and it was a shock to discover that they loved each other. Now they had to decide what they were going to do and if they had a future together.

The thought was like a blast of ice cold air. Ben shivered as he abruptly let her go. How had he allowed himself to forget that he might not have a future? Pain ran through him. Maybe they did love each other but it wasn't a guarantee that they'd live happily ever after.

'Ben? What is it? What's wrong?'

The alarm in her voice made him hate himself even more. Hadn't he done enough by running out on her when she'd needed him without adding this? He shook his head, knowing that he couldn't allow the situation to deteriorate any further.

'Nothing. I just don't think we should rush things.'

'Not rush things?' she repeated incredulously. 'We've spent the last three years apart and now we've realised that we love each other. I don't think anyone would blame us for *rushing things*!'

'Maybe not but we need to think everything through first.'

'This has all to do with your cancer returning, hasn't it?'

Ben flinched when he heard the fear in her voice. He couldn't bear to know that he was responsible for it. 'We have to face facts, Emily, and the most important fact of all is that I can't promise to be here for you for ever.'

'Nobody can promise that,' she said, her voice catching. 'If we're facing facts, then I can't promise to be here for ever for you, either, Ben.'

He sighed. 'It's not the same. The chances of something happening to you are far less than they are of it happening to me.' He held up his hand when she went to speak. 'It's true, Emily. At the moment I am free of cancer and have been for the past five years. To all effects, I'm cured but there's always a chance that I could relapse at some point. I know what it did to my parents when I was ill—how they suffered—and I don't want you and Theo to have to go through all that.'

'I understand that, but you may not relapse. You could remain fit and healthy.' She caught hold of his hands, holding them tightly in hers as though she could convince by touch. 'Don't cut us out of your life because of something that may never happen, Ben. It's crazy to do that.'

Ben didn't know what to do. He wanted to believe

what she was saying, but the doubts were too deeply entrenched. There was just no guarantee that the cancer wouldn't return. It might not be this week, this month, or this year even, but it could happen. The thought of putting her through that sort of heartache was more than he could stand, so it was a relief when Theo appeared, holding his new car. He showed it to Ben and smiled.

'Come and play, Ben.'

Emily fixed a smile to her mouth as she released him and turned to the little boy. 'Why don't you fetch some more of your cars downstairs, darling, then you and Ben can have a proper game?'

Theo nodded happily as he turned and ran back down the hall. Ben watched him go with an ache in his heart the size of a mountain. If he did the right thing and walked away, this might be the only chance he got to spend time with his son.

'Go on through to the sitting room. Theo won't be long.'

Emily whisked the plates off the table. Turning on the tap, she filled the bowl with water. Ben hesitated, wanting to say something to make her feel better, but there wasn't anything he could think of. He made his way to the sitting room, forcing himself to smile when Theo came charging in with a shoebox full of toy cars. He tipped them onto the rug then looked expectantly up at him.

'Shall we play races?' Ben suggested, crouching down. He took a bright blue car out of the pile and, with the addition of appropriate engine noises, propelled it across the rug. Theo laughed as he picked up his new

car and sent it hurtling after Ben's. The resulting crash
had him chortling in delight and Ben smiled sadly. He
didn't want this to be a one-off. He wanted to play with
Theo night after night but would it be right? Would it
be fair? Until he was sure about what he was doing, he
had to hold back.

Despair filled him. He didn't want to risk breaking
Theo's heart as well as Emily's, so help him.

Emily draped the tea towel over the radiator then took
a deep breath. She had managed to spin out the wash-
ing up for as long as she could and now it was time to
face Ben. She could hear Theo laughing as she made
her way down the hall and felt pain wash over her. It
was obvious that Theo had taken a shine to Ben and
she couldn't bear to think that this might be the only
opportunity her son had to spend any time with him.
She had to convince Ben that he was making a mistake
by cutting himself off from them. Maybe he couldn't
promise to be around for ever, but he was here now and
that was what mattered.

The thought of a time when Ben might not be around
was too hard to deal with and she pushed it to the back
of her mind. Pausing in the doorway, she took in the
scene. Ben was lying, full length, on the rug, using
his legs to create a tunnel for Theo to drive his cars
through. It was obvious that they were both enjoying
themselves hugely and her heart contracted. Maybe
Theo didn't know that Ben was his father but there
was definitely a connection between them.

'Looks like you two are having fun,' she said

brightly. She smiled at Theo, not wanting him to suspect anything was wrong. 'Poor Ben must be worn out, pretending to be a tunnel.'

'I don't mind.'

Ben's voice grated and Emily knew that he'd been thinking the same thing. Ben didn't like the thought of this being a one-off any more than she did. The realisation reinforced her decision to convince him that it was wrong to cut himself off from them. Maybe it was the noble thing to do but she didn't give a damn about that. Theo needed to get to know his father and the only way he'd do that was by spending time with him!

'Good, because it looks as though you've got yourself a permanent job.'

Ben's eyes darkened when he heard the challenge in her voice although he didn't say anything. Emily smiled sweetly then turned to Theo. If this was to be a battle of wills then she was more than happy to employ whatever tactics were necessary to win. 'It's time for bed now, darling. Put your cars away and then you can have your bath.'

'Want to play with Ben,' Theo muttered, his lower lip jutting ominously.

'Another time, sweetheart.' Emily scooped up several cars and popped them into the box. She shook her head when Theo immediately tipped them onto the floor again. 'No, that's naughty. It's time to tidy up ready for bed.'

'No!' Theo picked up a car and threw it across the room.

'Stop it.' Emily knelt down in front of him. 'If you're

going to be a naughty boy then you'll have to sit on the naughty step.'

Theo ignored her as he reached for another car and flung it across the room. Emily took hold of his hand and led him out of the room, sitting him down on the bottom step. Tears were streaming down his face but she knew that if she gave in then she would be asking for trouble in the future.

'You're to sit there until you can behave properly. Understand?'

Theo let out an angry roar as she went back to the sitting room. Ben was on his feet, looking worried.

'Is it because I'm here?'

'No. Just a touch of the terrible twos.' She smiled when he looked puzzled. 'A lot of two-year-olds have tantrums. Theo will soon calm down, you'll see.'

He grimaced. 'I have a lot to learn.'

'All parents do, assuming they're prepared to put in the time and effort.'

He sighed. 'I want to, Emily. I want to more than anything.'

'Then do it. Don't let anything put you off.' She looked into his eyes, praying that she could convince him to see sense. Now that they had found each other again, she couldn't bear to think that this might be the end. 'You can be a father to Theo if it's what you really want.' She paused but the words had to be said. 'We can be a proper family, if that's what you want too.'

CHAPTER TEN

A PROPER family.

Ben could feel the words reverberating inside his head. He barely noticed when Emily excused herself to go to Theo. Sinking down onto the sofa, he tried to rid his mind of the tantalising thought but it refused to budge. A proper family—was that what he wanted? Him, Emily and Theo?

He'd been too involved with his career before the cancer had struck to think about having a family and afterwards he had simply ruled out the idea of it happening. Now Emily's words had opened up a whole new world to him, one, he realised, that he wanted to grab with both hands, but how could he? How could he commit himself to having a family when he had no idea how long he had left on this earth?

Pain seared through him and he closed his eyes. Although he'd thought he had accepted that his future was uncertain, that had been before he'd met Emily again. Now he found himself cursing fate for dealing him such a rotten hand. It would almost have been better if he'd been told that he had X number of years to live; at least then he could have made his plans accordingly. However, this ongoing uncertainty made him feel as though he was in a state of limbo. *If* he remained free of cancer he could have everything he'd ever dreamt about. But *if* it came back, he'd have even more to lose. Could he really live with that prospect?

'Theo wants to say goodnight.'

Emily came back with Theo and Ben's heart contracted as he opened his eyes. How he longed to be part of their lives. He would be the happiest man alive if he could do that.

'Goodnight, Theo.' He stood up and went over to them, bending so that he could look at the little boy—his son. His heart spasmed again so that it was all he could do to speak. 'I enjoyed playing with you, tonight, *mon petit.*'

'Theo enjoyed playing with you too, didn't you, darling? Let's hope you and Ben can do it again very soon.'

Ben heard the challenge in Emily's voice and bit back a sigh. She was determined to get her own way but she didn't understand what it could mean. He only had to recall how his parents had suffered to know that he couldn't bear to put her and Theo through that kind of heartache.

'We shall see.' He ruffled the little boy's dark curls, ignoring the sharp look that Emily gave him. He wouldn't make any promises that he might not be able to keep.

'I'm sure we'll work something out,' she said firmly. She led Theo to the door then glanced back. 'Help yourself to more coffee. There's plenty in the pot.'

'Thank you but I think it's time I went.' He shrugged. 'You need to get Theo to bed so I'll get out of your way.'

'You don't have to leave,' she said quickly. 'I won't be long. Please stay.'

Ben shuddered when he heard the invitation in her voice. He knew that if he stayed he would end up spending the night with her. Even though it was what he longed to do, it wouldn't be right. Unless he could offer Emily what she deserved, a lifetime's commitment, then he wouldn't take advantage of her feelings for him.

'Thank you but I should go.' He looked her straight in the eyes, wanting there to be no mistake about his meaning. 'It's better this way, Emily. Believe me.'

'If you say so.'

She turned away without another word. Ben waited until she and Theo had gone upstairs before he let himself out. He got in the car, feeling the pain tugging at his heart. He didn't want to leave, but he didn't have a choice. He had to go or he would run the risk of hurting Emily and Theo and that was something he refused to do. As he drove back to Bride's Bay, he could feel an emptiness opening up inside him. Maybe he couldn't have that family Emily had spoken of but he could imagine how wonderful it would have been. He, Emily and their son together. For ever.

Emily felt worn out when she arrived at the surgery the following morning. She'd spent a sleepless night thinking about everything Ben had said. Although she believed he was wrong to cut her and Theo out of his life, she had no idea how she could persuade him to reconsider. He was determined to do the noble thing, no matter what it cost him. Or her.

Tears welled to her eyes as she hurried into her room. Closing the door, she went over to the washbasin and splashed her face with cold water. She had just finished when Hannah appeared.

'Hi, Emily. I was wondering if you could squeeze Mitch Johnson in for a blood pressure test this morning,' she began then paused uncertainly. 'Are you all right? You look as though you've been crying.'

'I'm fine.' Emily summoned a smile as she went over to the desk and checked her diary. 'I can fit Mitch in around eleven if that's any use.'

'That would be great. Thanks,' Hannah replied automatically then sighed. 'Look, tell me to mind my own business if you like, but has something happened? Between you and Ben, I mean?'

'Yes and no.' Emily dredged up another smile but she could feel her eyes filling again. 'He came to see Theo last night.'

'He told us you'd invited him round. Did things not go too well?'

'No, it was fine. Theo seemed to take a real shine to him in fact.'

'So what's the problem?'

'The problem is that Ben has decided it would be better if he didn't get involved in Theo's life after all.'

'What!' Hannah exclaimed. 'Why on earth not?'

'Because he's worried about Theo getting hurt if… if anything happens to him.'

A sob welled from her lips and Hannah hurried over

and put her arm around her. 'Come and sit down and tell me all about it.' She steered Emily towards the couch and sat her down then drew up a chair. 'Come on. Give.'

Emily found herself pouring out the whole sorry tale. 'Ben's decided that it would be wrong to get involved in case the cancer comes back. I tried to convince him that he was making a mistake but he seems determined to do things his way.'

'I see.' Hannah sighed. 'It's a very difficult situation, isn't it? I don't know how I'd feel if I were in Ben's shoes.'

'You wouldn't turn your back on the people who love you!' Emily countered hotly and Hannah's brows rose.

'Are you saying what I think you are?'

'That I love Ben?' Emily shrugged. 'Yes, I do. He also admitted that he loves me but apparently it's not enough to make him see sense.'

'Oh, Emily, I am *so* sorry. I don't know what to say, really I don't.' Hannah got up and gave her a hug. 'Do you want me to ask Tom to have a word with him?'

'No thanks. Apart from the fact that I doubt if it would achieve anything, it's something we have to sort out for ourselves. If Ben doesn't love me enough to overcome his fears, there's not much I can do.'

'I doubt if it's a lack of love that's causing the problem. Just the opposite, I'd guess.' Hannah stood up. 'I know it's hard, Emily, but don't give up just yet, will you? Ben may change his mind.'

'I doubt it.'

They didn't say anything more on the subject. However, the thought that Ben might change his mind lingered for the rest of the day. Emily knew that she had to do as her friend had suggested and not give up. Maybe it was a long shot, and maybe she wouldn't be able to persuade him to see sense, but she had to try. She would always regret it if she didn't.

In contrast to the previous day, Ben found the time dragged. Not even the patients could take his mind off the thoughts that had plagued him ever since he'd left Emily's house the night before. Was he making a mistake by turning his back on her and Theo? Would Theo come to hate him for not being a proper father to him? But what would happen to them both if the cancer returned and he needed more treatment?

By the end of the day, his head was aching from worrying about it. All he wanted to do was to go home, not home to Tom and Hannah's house, but home to his apartment in Paris. He was convinced that once he was back there, he would be able to think things through and decide what to do. Being so close to Emily only complicated matters.

As soon as he left the surgery, he phoned the airline and booked himself onto a flight leaving on Saturday morning. Obviously, he couldn't go before then when he'd promised to fill in for Simon but he should be able to get through another couple of days. He felt a little better by the time he drew up in front of Tom and Hannah's cottage, calmer, less stressed. Hannah was coming out of the sitting room when he let himself in and he smiled at her.

'You were quick tonight.'

'My list was a bit shorter than usual so I was able to

get away on time for once.' She glanced round when the door bell rang. 'Oh, that must be Emily. She offered to fetch Charlie from nursery when she collected Theo and drop him off on her way home.'

Ben didn't have time to do anything before she opened the door. Emily was standing on the step, holding Charlie. She had Theo with her as well and he felt his heart ache as he looked at them, the two most important people in his life. How could he walk away and leave them, yet how could he stay and possibly end up hurting them?

'Hello, Ben. How are you?'

Emily's voice was low, the smile she gave him filled with the same uncertainty that filled him, and his heart overflowed with both tenderness and pain. Whatever he did, Emily would get hurt and he couldn't bear to think of her suffering.

'Confused.' He returned her smile, knowing that she could see everything he was feeling.

'Me too.' She handed Charlie to Hannah, who diplomatically took him into the sitting room, leaving them alone. 'All I can think of is that there has to be a way through this, a way that doesn't mean you cutting us out of your life.'

'I don't want to cut you out, Emily. Really I don't,' he admitted, unable to lie.

'Then don't. I know you're afraid of us getting hurt, but we're hurting now, Ben.' She glanced at Theo. 'Theo must have asked at least a dozen times on the drive here if you were coming for supper. You've made a big impression on him.'

'Have I?' Ben's heart swelled with joy at the thought that he had already formed a bond with the child. He bent and ruffled Theo's hair. 'Have you had a good day at nursery, *mon petit*?'

'Yes. I took my new car.'

Theo proudly showed him the red racing car that Ben had bought for him, making it clear that it was his most prized possession, and Ben's heart swelled that bit more. Straightening up, he looked at Emily, knowing that he was allowing his emotions to get the better of him yet unable to stop it happening. 'May I come for supper again some time?'

'You can come tonight, if you want to,' she said softly. 'It will be pot luck, I'm afraid, but you won't starve.'

'I don't care.' He shrugged. 'It is not the food that interests me but the people who will be there.'

She smiled up at him, her pretty face alight with laughter. 'You always did know how to pay the most wonderful compliments. You must practise them!'

He laughed, thrilled to see the warmth in her eyes that had chased away that expression of despondency. 'Are you accusing me of being a flirt, Miss Jackson?'

'Yes. I'm sure you flirt with all the women who pass through your life.'

'I do.' He sighed. 'Particularly the older ladies. A little harmless flirting does a lot to restore a person's spirits, I find.'

'It certainly gave mine a boost,' she said, laughing. She grasped Theo by the hand. 'Come on, darling, it's time we went home. Ben's coming for supper and I need to see what's in the fridge.'

'Don't go to any trouble,' he said quickly. 'I'm happy with whatever you're having.'

She looked back and grinned. 'You may regret saying that!'

She was still laughing as she led Theo to the car and strapped him in. She sketched Ben a wave but for several minutes after she had driven off, he stayed where he was. He knew that supper would be just the precursor to a whole lot more and although the thought of making love to Emily filled him with joy, it also scared him. Once they'd moved their relationship up a notch, it would be so much harder to hold back.

'Fish fingers, chips and beans. Theo chose it. It's his favourite supper.'

Emily grinned at the bemused expression on Ben's face as she put the plate in front of him. She had half expected him to have second thoughts and cancel but she'd been wrong. He had arrived half an hour ago and spent the intervening time playing with Theo. Did it mean that he'd had a change of heart and intended to stick around? She had no idea, but it was a starting point, a stepping stone towards rebuilding their relationship.

Heat roared through her at the thought of all that it entailed and she hastily fetched her own plate. Theo was happily tucking into his supper, obviously eager to get back to the game he and Ben had been playing. She hadn't been lying when she'd told Ben that Theo had been asking about him; Ben's name had been mentioned so many times that she'd lost count. He had made a huge impression on Theo and that had to be a good thing... Didn't it?

A sliver of doubt wormed its way into her mind and she frowned. Was she right to push Ben into being a real father to Theo when there was a chance the child could get hurt? She'd been so intent on making Ben reconsider his decision that she'd not really thought it all through, but if Theo came to love Ben, as he would, it would break his heart if something happened to him.

Her head swirled with worry before common sense asserted itself. She was doing what all parents did, looking for dangers so they could prevent their child getting hurt. However, you couldn't wrap children in cotton wool; you had to let them live their lives to the full. And having Ben in his life would give Theo so much.

They finished their meal in record time. Ben placed his cutlery neatly on his plate and patted his stomach. 'Well, I have to confess that I never imagined fish had such tasty extremities. I shall have to add fish fingers to my menu.'

'That should please someone we know,' Emily replied, smiling. She gathered up their plates. 'Fruit and ice cream for pudding?'

'Sounds delicious,' he murmured, smiling back at her.

Emily nearly dropped the plates when she saw the desire simmering in his eyes. Although she had guessed how the evening might end, she hadn't expected it to advance so quickly! She put the plates on the worktop then hunted the ice cream out of the freezer. There were some late raspberries to go with it so she divided them between three dishes and added a scoop of ice cream.

'Ta-dah!' she said, carrying the dishes over to the table. 'This must be the easiest dessert ever.'

Ben scooped up a spoonful. 'And the most delicious.'

His tongue flicked out as he licked away a smear of ice cream that had lodged at the corner of his mouth and Emily's heart went into overdrive. She could feel it hammering away as she spooned up her own ice cream. How could such a seemingly innocent gesture be so erotic? It all depended on who was doing the lip licking, of course, and in this instance Ben had pole position.

Theo finished first, scraping the last smear of raspberry juice out of his dish. 'Finished, Mummy. Get down, please.'

'Just let me wipe your sticky mouth.' Emily swiped a wet wipe over his mouth then dropped a kiss on his lips, trying not to think about how much she longed to do the same to his father. 'Right, all clean so off you go.'

'Ben come too?' Theo demanded.

'In a moment, *mon petit*. I shall just finish my ice cream first.' Ben shook his head when Theo pleaded with him to come now. 'No. I shall come when I've finished, Theo. Okay?'

'Okay.'

Theo jumped down from the table, obviously realising that there was no point pursuing it, and Emily nodded approvingly.

'Thank you. Theo is very good but like most children, he does try to get his own way. I always try to be firm with him so he understands that no means no.'

'It's the only way he will learn,' Ben agreed. He popped the last raspberry into his mouth and sighed. 'That was delicious. Thank you.'

'Not really cordon bleu cooking, though, was it?' Emily replied wryly as she stood up to gather up their bowls.

Ben caught her hand and raised it to his lips, pressing an ice-cream-cold kiss to her knuckles. 'It didn't need to be. The company is what made it special.'

His voice grated, the heat it held such a contrast to the coolness of his lips that she shivered. Ben smiled as he let her go and stood up. 'I shall go and play with our son. No doubt he will beat me again. He's a devil when it comes to racing his toy cars.'

Emily leant against the table after he left the room, her whole body trembling. There wasn't a doubt in her mind about what was going to happen later. She closed her eyes, picturing her and Ben making love, shocked by how vivid the images were. For three years she'd tried—and succeeded—to block out thoughts like that, unable to bear being reminded of what a fool she'd been. But now she knew that Ben had and did love her, everything had changed. It hadn't been just sex then and it wouldn't be just sex tonight either. When they lay in one another's arms, they would be making love.

CHAPTER ELEVEN

BEN crept out of the bedroom. Pulling the door to, he paused but Theo was finally asleep. When the child had requested that Ben should put him to bed, Emily hadn't demurred. She had simply shown him where everything was kept and left him to it. For Ben, it had been a real joy to be able to play such a hands-on role and he appreciated the fact that Emily hadn't made a fuss about it. Another woman might have been wary of letting him bath Theo but she obviously trusted him and that meant a lot. That she was willing to trust him after the way he had behaved was more than he deserved.

Emily was sitting on the sofa, reading, when he went into the sitting room; she looked up and smiled. 'All quiet on the western front?'

'Indeed.' Ben laughed as he flopped down into a chair. 'Theo is all clean and shiny and he's had a story.'

'Just one?' Her brows rose. 'You did well if you got away with only one story.'

'Well, not quite. It did take a couple more before he settled down,' Ben admitted ruefully, and she laughed.

'More like ten if I know Theo! The last time he had a sleepover at my parents' house, Mum admitted that she read to him for over an hour before he dropped off to sleep. He can really hold out when he chooses to.'

'A very determined little fellow,' Ben said, grinning at her. 'Just like his mother.'

'Just like his father, you mean,' she countered pointedly, and he sighed.

'I am not trying to be stubborn, Emily. I just want to do what's right.'

'I know you do,' she said hurriedly, putting her book aside. 'Anyway, let's not talk about it now. How about some coffee to revive you after your travails in the bathroom?'

She went to get up but he leant over and caught her hand, pulling her towards him so that she ended up perched on his knees. 'I can think of something that would revive me far better than coffee,' he grated.

Dipping his head, he kissed her on the mouth, letting the passion that had been simmering inside him ignite. Maybe Emily had been trying to keep her own feelings damped down too because there was no hesitation about the way she responded.

Ben shuddered when he felt her mouth open under his. The feel and taste of her was doing all sorts of crazy things to his libido. She tasted so delicious, the faint tang of raspberries that lingered on her lips making his heart run wild. He could kiss her like this for ever and never grow tired!

He drew back at last, his breathing coming in laboured spurts that matched hers. They'd both been pushed almost beyond the limit, but he didn't care. Having her in his arms, feeling and tasting her was life affirming. 'How do you make me feel this way, *chérie*?' he murmured. 'I only have to touch you and rockets start going off inside my head, my heart starts racing, and as for breathing…' He shrugged, feeling his breathing worsen when the action made his chest brush against her breasts. Just feeling how her nipples immediately hardened was enough to drive even the sanest man wild and he wouldn't dream of placing himself in that category when he was with her.

'I don't know. If I did then maybe I could do something about the way I respond to you,' she said, nestling against him and thereby making the situation worse.

Ben could hear himself dragging in air like a sixty a day smoker and groaned. 'That would be a shame, though. If you worked out how to stop this magic happening, it wouldn't be the same.'

'No. It's much nicer this way, much better to just let it happen…' She pressed her mouth to his, letting her lips finish the sentence for her. Ben drew her to him, holding her so close that they were crushed together. He could feel every soft curve of her body against the hardness of his and his passion erupted. Standing up, he carried her to the sofa and laid her down then knelt beside her, his eyes tender as they drank in the flush on her cheeks, the brightness of her eyes. Emily loved him and wanted him and that was all he needed to know.

He undid her blouse, slowly, one button at a time, because there was no need to rush. They both knew how this would end and getting to the finish would be all the more delicious if they took their time. Her skin was warm, lightly tanned where the sun had touched it and pearly white where it had been sheltered from the elements. Ben ran his hands over her breasts after he'd freed them from the serviceable white bra. They too were warm, her skin smooth and soft, her nipples standing proud and erect when he ran his palms over them.

'You're so beautiful, *chérie*. So much of a woman that it makes me feel even more of a man.'

He kissed her nipples, slowly, tenderly, drawing them into his mouth so that he could savour their unique sweetness, and felt her shudder. When she started to unbutton his shirt, he sat quite still, allowing her to take the lead this time. She was quicker than him, more impatient to rid him of his clothes, but he didn't mind. If it pleased her that was fine by him.

She slid the shirt off his shoulders and stared at him, drinking in the tanned skin that was so much darker than her own. Lifting her hands, she traced the firm flat muscles, her palms grazing over his nipples so that they formed tight little buds. Ben closed his eyes, savouring the moment. Although he'd not been celibate for the past few years, nothing had happened in that time which had affected him the way Emily's touch was doing. Each light caress of her fingers branded him, marked him as hers, and he realised that it was what he wanted more than anything: for him to be hers and for her to be his. For ever.

The thought was too poignant. He had to make a conscious effort to hold it together otherwise he knew he would break down. That was the last thing he wanted to do, to spoil this and make her worry, to worry too. Maybe he was burying his head in the sand but who could blame him? This night had been a long time coming. He had never expected it would happen, in fact, and he was determined that it was going to be magical for both of them.

He tossed his shirt aside and finished undressing, uncaring that Emily could see from the aroused state of his body how much he wanted her. They weren't trying to hide anything or have secrets, they were making love. She slipped off her trousers and panties then held out her arms to him.

'Love me, Ben. Just love me.'

'I will. I do,' he murmured, moving over her. She was already wet and ready for him when he gently found the source of her heat so he wasted no more time. It wasn't necessary when they both needed this so much, needed to feel themselves joined in the most intimate act possible between a man and a woman.

Ben slid inside her, felt her close around him, and shut his eyes, blotting out everything but the sensations that were rippling through him. They were exquisite, raw and yet tender, such a mixture of feelings that it was impossible to describe each and every one. This was what love was all about, he thought, this feeling of flying, of reaching dizzying heights, of warmth and tenderness and caring. This was what made him know he was alive.

Emily shifted slowly, trying her best not to wake Ben, who was sleeping beside her. They had made love in the sitting room then again upstairs in her bedroom and the memory of what had happened that night would stay with her for the rest of her life. Ben had always been a caring and considerate lover but tonight he had been so much more. Tonight she had been given a rare glimpse of the man he kept hidden, a man who had so much love to give that it brought tears to her eyes to think about it. Ben had been holding back his emotions for so long because of the cancer but tonight they had come spilling out and she was only grateful that she'd been there to witness it.

'Emily?'

She turned towards him, loving the fact that when she looked into his eyes she could see that he loved her too. He had never allowed her to see his true feelings three years ago. She'd had to guess how he'd felt, assumed that he had cared for her and been devastated when it had appeared that she'd been wrong. Now, however, everything he felt was clear to see and she gloried in the fact that he trusted her enough not to hide behind a barrier any more.

'I was trying not to wake you,' she murmured, snuggling against him.

'*Pourquoi?* Why?' He ran a deceptively lazy hand down her body, tracing the swell of her breast, the dip of her waist, the curve of her hip, and she felt her passion ignite all over again. 'Don't tell me you are tired of me already, *chérie*. That would be so disappointing, especially as I have plans to…entertain you.'

Emily wriggled when his voice lingered seductively on the final words. She'd already had a taste of Ben's ideas on entertaining her and couldn't wait for it to happen again. She smiled, her lips brushing against the warm, hair-roughened skin on his chest. 'Oh, I'm not tired of you just yet.'

'Sure?' He tilted her chin so that he could look into her eyes and she couldn't fail to see the searching light in his.

'Quite sure. I can't imagine ever growing tired of you, either, Ben. You could find yourself entertaining me for a long time to come.'

'I wish.'

His tone was wistful although he didn't expand on the thought. Emily knew what he was thinking, though, and wished she hadn't said anything but they couldn't ignore the problems they might face even if they wanted to. Ben might not have a long time or he could have for ever. They just didn't know which it would be.

They made love again, slowly and with a depth of emotion that made them both cry. Emily knew that she had never experienced anything as profound as she did that night. It felt as though not only their bodies had been united but their souls too. If she'd thought she had loved Ben before then, she knew that she had barely scraped the surface of her feelings for him. He was her heart, her soul, the person she wanted to be with for ever.

The sun was just slanting through the window when they got up. It was almost six a.m. and in another half hour, Theo would be awake. By tacit consent they had both decided it would be better if Theo didn't find Ben there when he woke in case it confused him. Ben showered first while she made them a cup of tea. He came into the kitchen, his hair still damp, his jaw dark with morning beard, and Emily smiled at him.

'I should have given you one of my razors so you look less like a pirate.'

'And what's wrong with looking like a pirate?' he demanded, coming over and wrapping his arms around her. He rubbed his chin against her cheek, laughing when she tried to push him away.

'Stop it! I'll have whisker burns on my face.'

'Tut, tut, that will never do.' He dropped a kiss on the nape of her neck then let her go and picked up his tea. 'How would you explain that to your patients, I wonder?'

'Never mind my patients, how would I explain it to Theo? And to my mother?' She groaned. 'Theo and I are going to my parents' house for tea tonight and Mum has eyes like a hawk. If there's even a trace of a whisker burn, she'll spot it!'

'What do you plan to tell them about me?' Ben asked neutrally.

'The truth.' She shrugged when he looked at her. 'I won't lie about what's happened, Ben. They already know that you're here in Bride's Bay and I intend to tell them the truth about what's happened. The problem is that they will want to meet you. Do you think you can handle it?'

'I would find it strange if they didn't want to meet me in the circumstances.' He sighed. 'They must have a very poor opinion of me.'

'I explained what happened,' she assured him. 'And once they meet you, everything will be fine. They're nice people, Ben, kind people. They won't try to make life difficult for you,' she told him, mentally crossing her fingers that her father would be able to resist giving Ben a piece of his mind.

'I'm sure they are nice people but I let you down, Emily. I know how I'd feel if anyone did that to my daughter. Then there's the fact that I may let you down in the future. That will hardly endear me to them.'

'Don't say that! They will be fine—honestly.'

She kissed him on the mouth, wanting to convince him, but she could tell she hadn't succeeded. He drew back and checked his watch then put down his mug.

'I'd better go. I need to get changed for work and Theo will be awake soon. I'll see you at the surgery. All right?'

'Of course.'

Emily saw him out although she didn't linger. She could hear Theo stirring and needed to get a move on. However, as she ran up the stairs, she realised that not even the night they had spent together had rid Ben of his doubts about the future. All she could hope was that it had gone some way towards making him see that they could have a life together if it was what he wanted as much as she did.

It was lunchtime before Ben had a chance to speak to Emily. In a way, he was relieved because he'd needed breathing space. The previous night had been so wonderful that it would have been all too easy to assume that everything was fine, but he knew it was far from being that. Making love with Emily had merely reinforced his doubts about what they were doing. He loved her so much and she obviously loved him too but no amount of love guaranteed a happy ending. If anything happened to him then she would be hurt beyond belief and he couldn't bear to imagine her suffering.

She was in the staffroom making coffee when he popped his head round the door. She glanced up and Ben felt his heart lift when he saw the love in her eyes. It took him all his time not to rush across the room and take her in his arms but he had to be strong, had to do the right thing, if he could.

'How about lunch out somewhere?' he suggested. It would be easier to talk on neutral ground, he decided. If they went back to her house then they would end up in bed again and whilst his heart raced at the thought, they needed to talk about the issue that was uppermost in both their minds. 'Lizzie said that you have a couple of hours off this afternoon and I'm not needed so why don't we play truant? We can drive along the coast and find a pub that serves lunch.'

'That would be nice.' She switched off the kettle and headed for the door then paused. 'I'm afraid I'll have to wear my uniform, though. I've not got anything to change into.'

'You look lovely whatever you wear,' he assured her and meant it.

Emily grinned at him. 'Hmm, I didn't know you had a thing for uniforms, Dr Legrange.'

'I don't.' Ben chuckled as he slid his hand around her waist and drew her to him. 'Not unless they're being modelled by you, anyway.'

He dropped a kiss on her lips, inwardly sighing because he had broken his own rules. He should be trying to maintain a sensible distance, not kissing her.

He followed her out of the room, waiting in the corridor while she fetched her bag. He wasn't sure what he was going to say. He had to point out the problems, of course, make her understand how precarious the future was. There was no point thinking it was going to be easy to persuade her to see things his way and he hated to think that he might upset her, but it had to be done. He really couldn't bear to think that he might ruin her and Theo's lives at some point.

Emily carried her glass over to a table and sat down. Ben was at the bar ordering their lunch—hot chicken salad for her and sausage and mash for him. Taking a sip of her lime and soda, she tried to calm herself down but the nerves that had started clamouring for attention on the drive there refused to be quieted. Ben had planned this outing not just because he wanted to spend time with her but because he wanted to talk to her. And she knew exactly what he intended to say too.

'It shouldn't be very long.'

He joined her at the table, making himself comfortable on the high-backed settle. Heat roared through her when his thigh brushed hers and she took a hasty swallow of her drink. Ben might be determined to get his own way but she was equally determined to get hers. She wouldn't allow anything to distract her from that objective either.

'This is nice.' He glanced around the bar, taking

stock of the old wooden furniture that must have been in use for many years. There were all sorts of interesting knick-knacks dotted about, mainly items with a nautical theme like the glass floats off an old fishing net, and he nodded approvingly. 'It's good to find a place that hasn't been styled to within an inch of its life. Most city bars are clones of each other. Once one designer jumps on a theme, the rest follow.'

'We're a bit behind the times in that respect. Most folk round here prefer tradition so the local pubs don't tend to jump on the band wagon.'

'I imagine the tourists prefer it too,' he suggested, taking a sip of his lemonade.

'They do.'

Emily took a sip of her own drink, feeling suddenly nervous. Would she be able to convince Ben that it would be madness to cut her and Theo out of his life? Maybe he believed it was for the best, but he was wrong. Theo needed him. *She* needed him. And somehow she had to make him understand that.

'Look, Ben...'

'Emily, I...'

They both spoke at once and stopped. Ben shrugged. 'You first.'

'All right.' Emily knew there was no point beating about the bush. 'I know you brought me here to try and persuade me to see things your way but it's not going to work. Cutting yourself off from Theo and me for whatever reason is madness.'

'I disagree. It's the only thing I can do that makes any sense.'

His tone was flat and she shivered. She'd known it would be hard to convince him, but she had hoped he would at least consider her argument. However, the unequivocal note in his voice made her realise that he had made up his mind.

'You think it's sensible to allow your son to grow up without a father?' she countered, knowing how much it would hurt him. But all was fair in love and war, so she hardened her heart.

'It's not what I want, Emily, but I don't have a choice.'

'Of course you have a choice!' She closed her mind to the pain in his voice. She was fighting for them, for their future, and she would do whatever it took. 'It's up to you what happens, Ben,' she said, deliberately goading him. '*You* and nobody else. We can be a family or you can go back to Paris and carry on with your life. Maybe that's what you really want, to do exactly what you choose without having to consider anyone else.' She shrugged. 'I mean, why would you wish to give up your comfortable life to take on the responsibility of bringing up a child?'

He muttered something under his breath and her brows rose. 'Sorry. I didn't catch that.'

'It's unrepeatable.' He glared at her but beneath the anger she could sense his pain and her heart ached for what he was going through. It took every scrap of willpower not to weaken.

'Hmm, most people find it difficult to face the truth.'

'It isn't the truth, Emily. You know it isn't!' He leant forward, his eyes blazing into hers. 'I can't stay with you and Theo because I refuse to hurt you.'

'But you'll hurt us by leaving.' Tears rose to her eyes. 'You'll definitely hurt me, Ben, if you go.'

'Don't!' He took her hand, pressing a kiss to her palm. 'I love you, Emily, and I only want what's best for you.'

'*You* are what's best for me. You being here for me and Theo,' she said brokenly.

'But for how long? A year, two?'

'You don't know how long it will be. That's the whole point. You could have years and years, a whole lifetime, in fact.' She squeezed his hand, desperate to make him see how stupid this was, how wrong. 'You're free from cancer at the moment, Ben, and you could remain that way.'

'I could,' he conceded, although she sensed he was merely paying lip service to her argument rather than truly believing it. It was a start, though, and she leapt on it.

'Then promise me that you'll think about your decision. Imagine how you'll feel if you cut yourself off from us and the cancer never returns. It would be such a tragedy, Ben, wouldn't it?'

'All right, I'll think about it.'

Their lunch arrived then so they let the subject drop. However, Emily knew that she still hadn't convinced him. Ben was determined to do what he deemed was right and she had no idea how to persuade him to change his mind…unless she spent as much time as possible with him, her and Theo that was. Ben would find it that much harder to walk away once he'd had a taste of what he would be missing.

The thought buoyed her up as they ate their lunch. Maybe they were underhand tactics but if they achieved the desired result, she didn't care. Starting this very minute, she was going to make Ben see what he would be giving up!

CHAPTER TWELVE

'THANKS, Mum. I know it's short notice and I really appreciate it.'

Emily finished her call and hung up. She had just secured an invitation for Ben to join her and Theo at her parents' house for tea. She went to find him, mentally crossing her fingers that the evening would go as well as she hoped. This was the first step in her plan to keep Ben in her life and she wanted it to work. Whilst she knew that she could rely on her mother to make Ben welcome, she wasn't as certain about her father. Maybe she should have a word with him and explain what she was doing?

Ben was in the office when she tracked him down. He smiled when she went in. 'It looks as though I'll be busy this evening. There's quite a long list.'

'Mine's not too bad, fortunately,' Emily explained as she reached for the notes that Lizzie had left for her. She glanced through them, trying not to make it too apparent how nervous she was. If Ben refused the invitation, it would be a lost opportunity and she couldn't afford to waste any time. He was due to return to Paris at the end of the week which meant she had just a couple of days to convince him to reconsider his decision.

The thought brought it home to her how urgent the situation was and she hurried on. 'I've just been speaking to my mother and she asked if you'd like to join us for tea tonight?'

'It's very kind of her but I wouldn't want to be a nuisance,' he said quietly.

'You aren't,' Emily assured him. 'Mum is dying to meet you and she might not get another chance before you return to Paris.'

'In that case, I'd be delighted to accept.'

'Good.' She smiled at him. 'Theo will be thrilled. He'll be able to show you the chickens. He really adores them.'

Ben laughed. 'Tea and a visit to the chickens sounds wonderful. Shall we go in my car? There doesn't seem much point in using both cars.'

'There doesn't,' Emily agreed, thinking how well everything was working out. If they went in Ben's car, he would have to drive them home afterwards. And once he was there then there was no reason why he couldn't stay the night.

Her stomach lurched at the thought of them spending another night together and she turned away. Her plan seemed to be working out extremely well so far. The more time she and Ben spent together, the harder he would find it to walk away.

The thought carried her through evening surgery. Not even Maxine Barnes, there to have her blood pressure checked before renewing her prescription for the

Pill, could dent her spirits. Maxine had another of her brood with her and the child was obviously suffering from impetigo the same as her older brother. Emily sighed as she checked the poor little mite over once she'd finished doing Maxine's BP. 'It's definitely impetigo, Maxine. Chanelle must have caught it off Josh. Didn't Dr Legrange explain how contagious it is?'

'Yes, he did.' Maxine snorted. 'But as I told him, I don't have the time to go boiling towels and bedding!'

'Then you'll need to be prepared for the rest of the children to catch it,' Emily said firmly. As a nurse practitioner she was qualified to prescribe a range of medications so she printed out a script for the child and handed it to Maxine. 'Make sure you use it as per instructions. If you notice any spots on the other children or yourself and your husband then you'll need to come back.'

'You mean I could catch it!' Maxine exclaimed in horror.

'Oh, yes. It's not just something that kids catch. Adults can get it as well.'

Maxine didn't say anything; however, she looked stunned as she left the room. Emily smiled to herself. Hopefully, the thought of catching impetigo herself would be the incentive Maxine needed to take proper precautions. She saw the rest of her patients then tidied up. Ben was waiting in the foyer for her. Lizzie was tidying the reception desk and she smiled at Emily.

'Ben tells me he's going to your mum's for tea,' she said, obviously curious about the invitation.

'That's right.' Emily took a deep breath. Maybe it

would be wiser not to say anything until she was sure that Ben was going to stick around, but she was tired of dissembling. He was Theo's father and it was about time everyone knew that. 'My parents are looking forward to meeting him at long last.'

'Really?' Lizzie said, eagerly.

'Yes.' Emily smiled, hoping that Ben wouldn't be annoyed about what she was doing. Maybe it would put more pressure on him but that was a good thing in her view. 'It's only to be expected that they want to meet Theo's father, isn't it?'

'I…erm… Yes, of course.' Lizzie looked taken aback by the revelation. She barely managed to reply when Emily wished her a cheery goodnight.

Emily led the way from the surgery, heading to her car first to collect Theo's seat. Ben took it off her and carried it over to his car. He placed it in the back then stepped aside.

'I'll let you fasten it in. I've not had any experience of how these things work.'

There was something in his voice that made Emily wonder if he'd guessed what she was doing and she flushed as she bent to the task. She secured the seat then straightened up. Ben looked at her levelly as she closed the car door.

'Why did you tell Lizzie that I'm Theo's father?'

'Because it's true—you are.' She went to walk round to the passenger side but he put his hand on her arm.

'And that was the only reason? It had nothing to do with the fact that I'll find it all the more difficult to leave once everyone knows?'

'Maybe.' She looked him straight in the eyes. 'I'll do whatever it takes to convince you that you're making a mistake by leaving us, Ben.'

He sighed. 'You're just making it harder for yourself, Emily. You know why I can't stay. I've explained it to you.'

'But it doesn't mean that I agree with you!' She captured his hand. 'I don't care if we have one year or twenty together. I want you to stay with Theo and me, Ben. We need you.'

'Even if it means that Theo could get hurt?' He shook his head when she didn't answer. 'No, that isn't what you want, either, Emily, is it? You don't want our son to suffer any more than I do. If I leave now then he'll be disappointed, but he'll soon get over it.'

'Maybe he will but I won't!'

'Yes, you will.' He tilted her face up. 'You'll meet someone else in time, someone who can offer you a proper future, and you'll be glad I made this decision. You deserve to be happy, Emily. You don't deserve to be constantly living on a knife edge, wondering if the cancer will come back.'

Emily could tell how pointless it was to argue with him. She got into the car, her spirits at an all-time low. Nothing would convince Ben he was wrong, it seemed. The next couple of days were all she was going to have and she could either spend them at loggerheads with him or use them to create some memories for the future.

Her heart caught. To only have her memories and not be able to actually touch or speak to him would be unbearably painful.

* * *

The evening went better than Ben had expected. Emily's mother made him very welcome without going overboard. Her father was more reserved, admittedly, but Ben respected him for that. After all, he had run out on Noel Jackson's beloved daughter when she'd needed him most of all; in his shoes, Ben would have felt the same. When Noel suggested a tour around the farm after tea, Ben agreed immediately. They needed to clear the air, although he wasn't sure if that would be possible in the circumstances.

Noel led the way, pointing out the farm shop as they passed it.

'It was Frances who suggested we should open a shop,' Noel explained. 'I wasn't keen on the idea but she insisted. She was right too because it generates a large percentage of our income, especially since we started making our own cheeses.'

'Emily told me that you've started making your own yoghurt as well,' Ben said, wondering when Noel would get to the point.

'That's right. It's going very well, too. One of the leading supermarkets is interested in stocking it. If it does well then it'll mean us having to expand, though, and that's something we need to think about. We don't want to get too big.'

'Finding the right balance must be difficult,' Ben suggested as they carried on.

'It is. Frances and I will have to talk about it and make sure we're singing from the same hymn sheet.' Noel looked at him. 'That's most important in any relationship. Making sure you're both pulling in the same direction is vital.'

'It is.' Ben sighed. 'Unfortunately, Emily and I seem to be pulling in opposite directions at the moment.'

'Because you aren't sure if you want to commit yourself,' Noel said bluntly.

'Yes, although it's not quite as straightforward as it appears. I take it that you know I had lymphoma?' He carried on when Noel nodded. 'My biggest fear is that it could come back at some point. I don't want Emily and Theo to have to go through what my parents did. And if it turns out that it can't be treated next time…' He shrugged.

'I see. So what you're saying is that you're trying to protect them.'

'That's right, although Emily doesn't see it that way, I'm afraid.'

'Of course she doesn't.' Noel shook his head. 'She loves you—that's obvious.'

'And I love her too,' Ben said quietly.

'Then all I can say is that I hope you can work things out.' Noel's tone was gruff as befitted a man more comfortable dealing with practical matters. 'Frances and I have been married for almost thirty years. We've had our ups and downs but we've got through the tough times by facing them together.'

'So you think I'm wrong to take this stance?' Ben said slowly.

'I've not been in your position so I'm not qualified to say. However, I'd advise you to think long and hard before you make up your mind. It's not just your life that will be affected but Emily's and Theo's as well.'

Noel didn't say anything more on the subject. Nevertheless, Ben knew that he would take the older man's advice on board. Was he making a mistake? Should he allow Emily to do what she so obviously wanted to do and be there for him? Should they face whatever the future brought together, like Noel and Frances Jackson had done?

It was tempting, so very, very tempting, and yet he couldn't quite bring himself to change his mind. He kept remembering his mother and how pale and drawn she'd become as she'd sat with him in the hospital. Then there was his father. Serge Legrange's heart problems had started shortly after Ben had finished his treatment. Ben had often wondered if the strain of watching his son go through that ordeal had had something to do with it. It was widely accepted that suffering some kind of trauma could have a detrimental effect on a person's health and there was no doubt that Serge had been devastated when he had found out that Ben had cancer.

He sighed as he followed Noel into the milking parlour. Although he was tempted, he couldn't put Emily through all that. The last thing he wanted was her becoming ill because of him.

It was almost nine p.m. before they left the farm. Frances had insisted that Theo should stay the night so Emily had put him to bed in the room she'd had when she was a child. She guessed that her mother was trying to give her and Ben some time on their own and was grateful. Although she'd not had a chance to explain what she was doing, she suspected that Frances had guessed. This was her way of helping and Emily appreciated it.

'Thanks again for having Theo tonight, Mum,' she said, kissing Frances on the cheek.

'Any time, darling. You know your father and I love having him stay with us.' Frances gave her a hug. She drew back and smiled at Ben. 'It's been really lovely to meet you at last, Ben. I do hope you'll come again very soon.'

'Thank you. You're very kind.' Ben kissed her mother on both cheeks then turned to her father and held out his hand. 'And thank you, too, sir. I promise you that I shall do my very best to sort things out.'

'That's all I ask.'

A look passed between the two men as they shook hands, which immediately aroused Emily's curiosity. Obviously something had been said during their walk and she was dying to know what it was. She followed Ben out to the car, curbing her impatience as she waved to her parents. Ben would tell her if he wanted to and there was no point pushing him.

They drove back to the main road, picking up speed once they were clear of the farm. There was quite a lot of traffic about, mainly tourists who were visiting the area. Ben slowed down, tucking in behind an old camper van which was making heavy weather of the hilly coastal road.

'I've not seen one of those vans for years,' he said,

changing down a gear. 'It's a miracle that it's still road-worthy.'

'Only just from the look of it,' Emily observed lightly. She grimaced when a cloud of exhaust fumes wafted through the open windows. 'Oh, yuk, that smells awful! It's burning oil by the gallon.'

'I didn't know your talents encompassed car mechanics,' Ben teased her as he rolled up the windows.

'I'm a farmer's daughter,' she retorted. 'I can strip a tractor engine with the best of them!'

'Really?' Ben laughed out loud. 'I know who to come to if my car breaks down then.'

'My fees are very reasonable,' she told him, laughing.

Ben smiled back, his eyes very dark as they lingered on her for a second. 'I shall be happy to pay whatever you charge.'

'I'm sure we can work something out,' Emily said softly, feeling her heart race. Maybe they were ostensibly discussing cars but she knew what was really going on.

She bit her lip as Ben overtook the van when they reached a straight section of road. Ben was going to stay the night again. Maybe he hadn't changed his mind about leaving but he had no more control over his emotions than she did. He loved her; he wanted her. It should have guaranteed that things would work out the way she wanted them to but she knew that it wouldn't. He was as determined as ever to leave and she had to accept that and not spoil what little time they had left by arguing with him.

It was a sobering thought, one that stayed with her

as they drove back to Bride's Bay. Ben pulled up outside the cottage and switched off the engine. 'Shall I come in, *chérie*?'

'Do you want to?'

'Oui.' He leant across the seat and kissed her. Drawing back he looked into her eyes. 'If it's what you want too.'

Emily knew that he was giving her a choice. She could invite him in, knowing that nothing had changed, or she could ask him to leave and he would abide by her wishes. It was up to her and although she knew that in the circumstances she should tell him to go she couldn't bring herself to do so. Opening the car door, she got out, turning the decision back on him. He could follow her if it was what he wanted or he could drive away.

Her heart was hammering so loudly as she walked up the path that she couldn't hear a thing, neither the sound of his footsteps nor the noise of the engine. It was only when she felt his hands on her shoulders that she knew he had followed her and felt herself melt. Maybe Ben felt he couldn't stay but there was no doubt at all that he loved her.

She stepped inside the hall then turned to him. He was already reaching for her so that their bodies met with a small jolt. Emily stared into his face, wanting to commit every line to memory. When he left all she would have were these pictures in her head and she needed them to be as clear as possible when they would have to last her a lifetime. Tears welled to her eyes and she heard him utter something under his breath but had no idea what and didn't care. Words wouldn't heal her aching heart; nothing would.

He drew her to him, stroking her hair as he pressed her face into the hollow of his shoulder. '*Je t'aime*, Emily. I love you.'

His voice broke and she knew that he was overcome by his emotions too. This was as hard for him as it was for her and the thought was what she needed to get her through the moment of despair. Ben was hurting and she wanted to help him, heal him, love him and care for him even if it couldn't be for ever.

'*Je t'aime*,' she whispered. 'I love you, too, Ben. So much.'

Standing on tiptoe, she pressed her mouth to his and kissed him with every tiny scrap of love she felt. His arms tightened around her, drawing her to him, holding her against his heart where she wanted to be. When he deepened the kiss, she gloried in the taste and feel of him. When they were together like this, nothing else mattered. There were no issues to resolve. They were just two people in love, two people who wanted— *needed*—to show each other how much they cared.

Ben swept her into his arms and carried her into the sitting room. Laying her down on the sofa, he knelt beside her. His hands were trembling as he smoothed her hair back from her face and she understood. This was a moment they would remember for the rest of their lives and he wanted it to be special, as it would be.

She drew him down to her, showering butterfly-soft kisses across his cheeks and brow. His skin was burning hot as though he was running a fever, the faint rasp of beard that was starting to appear making her lips tingle when she reached his jaw, and she shuddered. Having the licence to kiss him how she chose was a heady experience and she intended to make the most of it.

Her mouth slid down his throat, lingering on the pulse that was beating wildly beneath his skin. She could feel it racing, feel its rhythm start to seep into her, and felt suddenly dizzy with power. *She* had done this to him! *She* had made his pulse race, his breathing quicken. *She* had aroused his passion. No matter what happened in the future, at this moment Ben was hers!

They made love right there on the sofa as they had done the night before and, unbelievably, it was even more magical. Emily felt consumed by their passion, enveloped in their love for one another. Ben carried her with him as they scaled the heights together and she carried him with her when they came down to earth again. Even though their lovemaking had been unimaginably wonderful, reality was just as good, she thought as she lay in his arms afterwards. Being with Ben, under any circumstances, was what she wanted, what she needed. With him she felt fully alive; without him, it felt as though some vital part of her was missing. How could she let him go and subject herself to living half a life? Somehow, some way, she had to persuade him to stay!

CHAPTER THIRTEEN

BREAKFAST was a rushed affair the next morning. Ben knew that it was his fault they were so pushed for time. Inviting Emily to join him in the shower had, predictably, led to other things, and he, for one, wasn't sorry. Making love to Emily was like an addiction; the more times it happened, the more he wanted it to. How was he going to survive without her when he returned to Paris?

The thought weighed heavily on him as he drove them to the surgery. Emily was such a vital part of his life now, as essential to him as the air he breathed. He couldn't imagine being without her but that was what he would have to do if he was to protect her and Theo. His heart felt leaden as he drew up in the car park. There were just two days left of his stay and it wasn't nearly long enough. He needed more than a few hours, a lifetime, in fact. But how long would his life be? That was the question he couldn't answer. And while there was this uncertainty hanging over him, he had to do what was right and not what he wanted.

'Just made it,' Emily declared, reaching for the door handle. She paused when he didn't answer. 'Ben? Are you okay?'

'Yes, I'm fine.' He summoned a smile, not wanting to get into a discussion about the future at that moment. Every time they spoke about it, Emily ended up in tears and it wasn't fair to upset her when they were about to go in to work. He got out of the car, waiting for her to join him so they could go into the surgery together. Now that the truth about him being Theo's father was out, there was no point pretending they weren't involved. Anyway, it was way past time that people knew how much he loved Emily even if at the end of the day he had to leave her.

He took her hand as they crossed the car park, feeling his heart ache at the thought of how empty his life would be without her and Theo. Opening the surgery door, he ushered her inside, summoning a smile for Lizzie who was tidying the magazines. '*Bonjour*, Lizzie. How are you today?'

'Very well, thank you.' Lizzie glanced from him to Emily and grinned. 'No need to ask how you two are this morning!'

Ben laughed. 'No need at all.' He let go of Emily's hand and smiled at her. 'I'll see you later, *chérie*. Enjoy your morning.'

'You too.'

Emily smiled at him with a world of love in her eyes and it was all he could do not to sweep her into his arms. He managed to control the urge and made his way to the consulting room instead. Booting up the computer, he checked his morning list, pleased to see that he had wall-to-wall appointments until lunchtime. At least if he was busy, he'd have less time to brood. He knew what he had to do and, painful though it was, he wouldn't go back on his decision. Come the weekend he would return to Paris and that would be it. Oh, he would keep in touch with Emily, of course, check how Theo was doing and try to persuade her to accept his help financially. However, as for their relationship, it would come to an end.

Ben closed his eyes, trying to envisage what his life would be like but it was impossible. Without Emily at its heart, the future was a blank canvas.

Emily was kept busy with appointments. There were several fasting blood tests booked in that morning so she did them first and parcelled up the samples ready for the courier to collect. The courier's van had just left when Simon appeared, looking unusually grave.

'Is something wrong?' she asked, following him across reception.

'Becky just phoned. Apparently the baby has had a febrile convulsion. She's at the hospital with her now, in fact.' Simon sighed. 'This is the last thing she needs on top of everything else that's happened.'

'It is,' Emily agreed sombrely. Simon's daughter, Becky, had had a rough time recently. She and her husband had been involved in a road traffic accident and sadly, Becky's husband had been killed. Becky herself had been badly injured so Simon and Ros had flown out to New Zealand to look after her and baby Millie, who fortunately hadn't been in the car at the time. This latest incident must be yet another blow for her.

'It must be difficult for her being so far away from you and Ros,' Emily said sympathetically.

'Which is why we're trying to persuade her to come back to England,' Simon explained. 'If she moved back here, we'd be able to help if there was a problem.'

'How does Becky feel about the idea?' Emily queried.

'I'm not sure.' Simon shrugged. 'She's become rather…well, *withdrawn* since the accident. She doesn't say much about anything to be honest.'

'It's understandable. I mean, losing her husband must be a lot for her to deal with,' Emily said quietly, trying not to see a parallel between what had happened to Becky and what could happen to her. How would she cope if Ben died? How would it affect Theo? Although she had thought about it before, she hadn't fully considered the implications and she had to admit that it was scary to imagine herself in Becky's position.

She went back to her room and worked her way through the rest of her list. It was mainly routine stuff—blood pressure checks, a couple who needed jabs before they went on holiday, a cervical smear. Emily did everything by the book, aware that her concentration wasn't as good as normal. Thoughts kept humming away in her head, unsettling and disturbing: could she cope if she and Ben were together and something happened to him? Would Theo cope if he lost the father he'd grown to love?

She realised that she needed to think about it properly instead of allowing her heart to rule her head. If it were just she who would get hurt then she was willing to take the risk, but was she prepared to risk Theo's happiness? Although she hated to admit it, it could turn out that Ben was right.

Ben switched off the computer, yawning widely as he stood up. It had been a busy day and he'd not had much sleep the previous night. Heat scorched along his veins as he recalled in graphic detail the reason why he'd spent so much of the night awake. Just remembering how it had felt to hold Emily in his arms, to stroke and caress her, made his body quicken and he groaned. He'd been right to think he was addicted to making love to her when like any addict he couldn't wait for his next fix!

He went to find her, pausing in the doorway to her room while he drank in the sight that met him. Emily was standing on a stool, reaching into the cupboard over the sink. The view of her rounded bottom snugly encased in those navy cotton trousers made a rush of desire surge through him. With or without clothes, Emily definitely had the power to stir him!

He must have made some sort of sound because she glanced round. 'Oh, I didn't know you were there.'

'I was enjoying the view, *chérie*,' he said, smiling at her.

A tide of colour flooded her face as she stepped down from the stool. 'Did you want something?'

'Not really,' Ben replied, somewhat surprised when she changed the subject. Usually, a remark like that would have been met with a pithy reply, but she seemed keen not to be drawn into that kind of conversation and he had to admit that he was puzzled. He went into the room, closing the door to afford them some privacy. 'Is something wrong, Emily?'

'Of course not!' She gave a tinkly laugh that sounded false to his ears. It must have sounded so to her too because she hurried on. 'I'll have to run, I'm afraid. I need to collect Theo from the nursery.'

'I thought he was staying at your parents' house,' Ben said levelly.

'No, Mum's taken him to nursery as usual. It's better if we stick to his routine,' she told him, taking her bag out of a drawer. She found her car keys then gave him a quick smile. 'I'll see you tomorrow.'

'Aren't you forgetting something?' Ben asked quietly, wondering what was going on. Emily seemed remarkably keen to get away from him and he had to admit that it stung to know that she didn't want to spend any time with him.

'I don't think so,' she said with a frown, glancing around.

'Theo's seat is still in my car,' Ben said flatly, suddenly impatient with himself. So Emily wasn't giving him one hundred percent attention; so what? She had Theo to think about and, quite rightly, his needs came first.

'Oh! You're right, I had forgotten.' She gave a little shrug as she headed for the door. 'Good job you remembered.'

She swished past him, heading briskly along the corridor. Ben followed more slowly, more convinced than ever that something was going on. Maybe Emily did have other things on her mind, but she'd never been so offhand with him before. He unlocked his car, shaking his head when she went to unfasten the child seat.

'I'll do it.' He carried it over to her car. Emily opened the rear door and he placed it in the back, leaving her to secure it in place. She gave him another of those overly bright smiles when she finished.

'That's it then. I'll see you tomorrow.'

'Have I done something to offend you?' Ben asked quickly, unable to bear the thought of them parting like this.

'Of course not!' She went to get into the car but he stopped her.

'Then why are you being so distant?' He bent and looked into her eyes. 'What's wrong, Emily? Something has upset you and I want to know what it is.'

She started to shake her head then stopped. Her face was grave when she continued. 'I realised today that I need to think about this situation and how it could affect Theo.'

'I see.' Ben felt his stomach sink which was an odd reaction when he had been urging her to do exactly that for the past week.

'If it were just me, then it would be different.' She touched his hand. 'I'd be willing to take the risk of getting hurt if it meant we could be together.'

'I know.' He turned his hand over, his fingers closing around hers although he wasn't sure if he was offering comfort or seeking it. 'But Theo's just a child. He needs us to look after him, Emily, and protect him.'

'Yes.' She bit her lip. 'It's so unfair, isn't it? We shouldn't be having to think about things like this. We should be getting on with our lives, getting on with being a *real* family.'

'We should, but that isn't possible, I'm afraid.' He let her go, afraid that if he didn't do so he wouldn't have the strength in a few more minutes. This was what he had wanted, for Emily to accept that it was impossible for them to be together, yet now that the truth had dawned on her, he felt completely gutted.

He opened the car door, waiting while she slid into the seat. She started the engine then looked at him and Ben could see the pain in her eyes. 'I love you, Ben. Please don't ever doubt that.'

'I won't.' He bent and kissed her. 'I love you too, *chérie*, more than life itself, which is why I can't bear to think of you getting hurt.'

She stroked his cheek. 'I'm old enough to cope with whatever life throws at us. If it were just you and me, Ben, then I wouldn't hesitate.'

'But it isn't only us. There's Theo to consider and neither of us wants him to suffer.'

Ben straightened abruptly, not needing her to answer because he knew how she felt. Emily couldn't bear to think of their child suffering any more than he could. He went back into the surgery, needing a few minutes to get his thoughts together. Emily had said that she needed to think about the situation but what was there to think about? If they stayed together and the cancer came back, Theo would suffer. However, if he left at the end of the week and broke off all but the most minimal contact, that wouldn't happen.

He took a deep breath, feeling the pain scoring deep

inside him. The solution to the problem would be as clear to Emily as it was to him.

Emily collected Theo but instead of going straight home, she went to her parents' house. Frances Jackson was just taking a casserole out of the oven when Emily let herself in. She took one look at her daughter's face and popped it back into the Aga.

'I'll put the kettle on,' she said, setting it on the hob. She smiled at her grandson. 'Gramps is in the milking parlour if you want to go and help him.' She took Theo by the hand when the little boy eagerly agreed and led him to the door. She paused and glanced at Emily. 'I'll just take Theo across to your father and come straight back, darling. All right?'

'Thanks, Mum.' Emily dredged up a smile. She fetched a couple of mugs and placed them on the table then put some tea bags into the pot. By the time her mother returned, the tea was ready.

'Tell me what's happened,' Frances instructed, shooing Emily towards a chair as she picked up the pot.

'I realised today that Ben was right,' Emily told her flatly. 'It would be better if we ended things.'

'You don't really mean that!' Frances exclaimed. She put the teapot down and stared at her. 'I thought you were determined to convince him that you could work things out?'

'I was, but I was wrong.'

'Why? I thought you loved him,' Frances challenged her.

'I do.' Emily grimaced, hoping the feeling of numbness that had enveloped her on the drive over would last. 'And I know Ben loves me, but that isn't the point.'

'Call me old-fashioned but I'd say that it *is* the point.' Frances shook her head. 'You two love one another and, I assume, you want to be together, so why on earth do you want to end things?'

'Because of Theo. He could get badly hurt and neither of us wants that.' Emily bit her lip as she felt pain pierce her heart. Obviously, the numbness had been a temporary state of affairs.

'You mean if Ben's cancer comes back and he dies,' Frances said bluntly and Emily winced.

'Yes.'

Frances sighed as she pulled out a chair and sat down. 'Darling, I know you want to protect Theo. You're his mother and it's your job to make sure that he's safe and happy but you can't wrap him in cotton wool. He has to learn how to deal with difficult and painful situations.'

'Having your father die isn't just a difficult situation, though, is it?' Emily retorted.

'No. It must be a terrible experience for any child to go through. But children are very resilient. They can and do cope with all sorts of dreadful things. I'm sure that Theo would cope too if something happened to Ben.'

'Do you honestly believe that?' Emily said slowly, feeling a little bubble of hope surface. 'You aren't just saying that to be kind?'

'No, I'm not. I love Theo and if I thought this could cause him untold harm then I'd be the first to agree that you were doing the right thing. But I know he will cope if the worst happens.' Frances patted her hand. 'I'm more worried about you, darling. I know how much Ben means to you.'

'I love him so much, mum,' Emily admitted. 'The thought of him dying is more than I can bear.'

'I understand that. But Ben is fit and healthy at the moment, isn't he? There's no reason to believe that the cancer will come back.'

'You're right.' Emily felt as though a weight had been lifted off her shoulders. She smiled at her mother. 'I let it all get on top of me. Simon was talking about Becky today and it brought it home to me how awful it must be to lose the person you love.'

'It's only natural, darling. I worry about your father, too, especially now that we're getting older,' Frances admitted.

'I never realised,' Emily said, guiltily.

'Good. The last thing I want is you worrying unnecessarily,' Frances said sternly.

Emily laughed. 'Still trying to protect me?'

'Of course. I'm your mother and it's my job to protect you even if you are all grown up!'

They both laughed and it broke the tension. Emily agreed to stay for supper and went to tell her father it was ready while Frances dished up. As she crossed the farmyard she realised in relief that it had been a temporary wobble and that she no longer had any doubts. Theo would gain so much from having Ben around and it would far outweigh everything else. Now all she needed to do was convince Ben.

Her heart lurched. Would he agree with her though,

or would he continue to believe that the only way was his way? Come Saturday he was due to leave and that would be the end for them if she didn't manage to convince him he was wrong. She squared her shoulders. She had just over twenty-four hours to bring him round to her way of thinking, which meant she had to make every second count. She was going to have to pay Ben a visit on her way home!

Ben switched off the television. Tom and Hannah had gone out for dinner and he was on his own. They had invited him to go with them but he'd refused, using the excuse that he had paperwork to do. It wasn't a lie; there was paperwork that needed doing, but it could wait until he got back to Paris. He simply couldn't face the thought of making conversation when his heart wasn't in it.

He stood up, too strung up to sit any longer. Knowing that Emily had come round to his way of thinking should have been a relief but it wasn't. He kept thinking about how empty his life was going to be without her and Theo even though he knew how selfish it was. Maybe a walk would help, he thought as he went to fetch his jacket. A bit of physical exercise should help him prioritise what was really important.

It was growing dusk as Ben made his way to the harbour. There were several fishing boats preparing to set sail and he stopped to watch them. The sound of the men's voices carrying on the breeze reminded him of holidays he'd had as a child on the French coast. Even though the fishermen there had spoken a different language they had made the same preparations, taken the same precautions before setting sail. Weighing up the risks was key.

He sighed. Emily had obviously weighed up the risks of them being together and decided against it. It was what he'd advocated yet it hurt to know that she felt Theo would be better off without him. Maybe he was being contrary but his cancer might never come back. In which case, he'd have lost his one and only opportunity to be a father to Theo and a husband to her. All of a sudden, he could see the situation from the other side and he cursed roundly. He should never have taken such a hard line!

'There you are. I wondered where you'd got to.'

Ben swung round when he heard Emily's voice. His heart leapt when she held out her hand. Maybe it was the poor light but he would swear that the doubts he'd seen in her eyes earlier had disappeared. 'Come on.'

Ben automatically took her hand as she headed back to the road. 'Where are we going?' he asked, his voice sounding hoarse.

'Home.' She stopped and looked to him. 'Theo's spending the night with my parents again so we'll have the house to ourselves.'

'But you said…'

'I know.' She rose on tiptoe and kissed him, effectively stopping his protest. She drew back. 'I know what I said, Ben. I know why I said it too. I was having a bit of a wobble but not any more. Theo needs you. *I* need you. Having you in our lives is the best thing that could ever happen to us. Now all I have to do is convince you.'

Ben knew he should object. He knew that he should

set out all the reasons why it would be better if he removed himself from her life for good. He knew what he *should* do but he realised that he wasn't going to do it. He pulled her into his arms and kissed her right there in the middle of the street, uncaring that there were people staring at them. He didn't give a damn about anyone else; he only cared about Emily. He loved her, wanted her, and even though his head said no, his heart said yes, yes, yes!

They walked back to her car in silence. Words weren't necessary when they each knew how the other felt. Ben could feel the excitement building inside him and knew that the same thing was happening to her. They had no problems when they were making love and maybe it was through their lovemaking that they would find a solution to this problem. He was willing to be convinced, eager to be swayed by her arguments, desperate to have what she was offering him—a future with her and Theo. His heart overflowed with joy. He couldn't imagine anything more wonderful than that!

CHAPTER FOURTEEN

MOONLIGHT streamed through the window, casting a silvery glow over the room. Emily watched the play of light and shadow on Ben's face. Even though she couldn't read his expression, she knew how he felt, that he loved her with the whole of his heart, and joy enveloped her. It was going to be all right! Ben was going to stay. He could no more walk away and leave her and Theo than she could have done.

She kissed him, softly, lingeringly, and heard him sigh. Running the palms of her hands down the strong column of his back, she urged him closer. Tonight their lovemaking was taking on a different role. It wasn't just a way to express their love, it was putting the seal on their future. After all the heartache and uncertainty it was almost too much to believe that what she had hoped for had come true.

'I love you, my darling.'

Ben's voice vibrated with emotion and Emily shivered. To know that he loved her this much was humbling. She closed her eyes, feeling the sensations build inside her as he entered her. Making love with Ben had never been just a purely physical experience and tonight it was so much more again. It was a promise for their life together as well as an expression of their love. No matter what happened, they would be there for one another, as they would be there for Theo. For the first time since Ben had come back into her life, Emily was sure that they were united in their objectives.

They lay side by side afterwards, their hands touching because neither of them could bear to lose all contact. Emily sighed softly, wishing the night would never end. Ben turned, a frown drawing his brows together as he looked at her.

'Why did you sigh? Is something wrong, *chérie*?'

'No. Far from it.' She smoothed away the frown lines with the tip of her finger. 'I sighed because I never want tonight to end.'

'Me too,' he murmured, leaning over so he could kiss her. He drew back and smiled. 'Although I have to confess that I feel like that every time we make love. I always wish the night would never end!'

'Do you?' Emily laughed. 'Good. Long may it continue.'

'Oh, I can't imagine that my feelings will change,' he assured her.

Emily rolled onto her side and rested her hand on his chest. She could feel his heart beating beneath her palm and drew reassurance from the heavy, steady rhythm. 'So am I right to think that you've changed your mind and are going to stay?'

'*Oui*. Although we shall need to work out the practicalities, of course.' He took her hand, pressing a kiss to her palm before placing it back where it had been. He grimaced. 'I shall have to return to Paris, unfortunately, because I'm needed at the clinic. I wish I could stay here with you and Theo but it isn't possible right now.'

'I understand, Ben, really I do.' She smiled at him. 'I know how important the clinic is to you and I don't expect you to abandon it for us.'

'In that case, would you consider moving to Paris if only on a temporary basis?' He shrugged. 'Once the clinic is running smoothly then we can decide where to live. But at the moment, I need to be there to orga-nise things.'

'I shall definitely think about it,' Emily said slowly. 'It would mean uprooting Theo, but he's still very young—I'm sure he'd soon adapt to living somewhere else.'

'It would mean you moving away from your parents, though, Emily. I know how close you are to them so do you think you could bear it?'

'If it means we can be together then yes,' she said, coming to a swift decision. After all the worry about losing Ben, moving to Paris didn't seem like such a big deal. She smiled at him. 'Anyway it's not as though Paris is a million miles away. It's just an hour's flight so Mum and Dad can always visit us.'

'Of course they can.' Ben pulled her to him and hugged her. 'I can't believe that you're willing to give up your life here to be with me.'

'It's no hardship,' she assured him. She kissed him lightly on the mouth then grinned. 'The question is whether you'll be able to put up with having Theo and me around on a permanent basis.'

'It won't be easy but I'll manage—somehow!' he told her, laughing when she grabbed a pillow and swatted him with it.

The ensuing tussle ended, predictably, with them making love again. As Emily drifted off to sleep some time later, she knew that she would never forget this night. It was the night when all her dreams had finally come true. She felt as though she should pinch herself to make sure she wasn't *really* dreaming, but then she glanced at Ben, lying beside her, and realised it wasn't a dream after all. She and Ben were going to be together. For ever.

Simon insisted that Ben and Emily should take Friday afternoon off so they collected Theo from the nursery and took him to the beach. The little boy was almost giddy with excitement as he raced across the sand, shouting for Ben to come and paddle with him. Ben laughed as he kicked off his shoes.

'It appears I'm needed.'

'Have fun.' Emily spread the travel rug over the sand. She sighed luxuriously as she sat down. 'I'll just sit here and sunbathe while you entertain him.'

'No way!' Ben scooped her up and headed towards the sea, laughing when she tried to wriggle free. 'If we're going paddling then so are you!'

Emily squealed when he deposited her in the shallows. 'My sandals are soaked now!'

'You should have taken them off, shouldn't you,' he said with a grin, turning to Theo. 'Silly Mummy.

Fancy forgetting to take off her sandals before she went paddling.'

'Silly Mummy,' Theo repeated, laughing delightedly. Bending down he splashed them both with water, shrieking with excitement when Ben grabbed hold of him and swung him up into the air.

'I think someone needs a ducking,' Ben said, turning him upside down so that Theo's hair just touched the waves.

'Again! Again!' Theo demanded so Ben did it again then placed him carefully back on his feet. He groaned when Theo immediately scooped up another handful of water and showered him with it.

'Oh, no. Not again!'

Emily laughed as she moved out of the way. 'You deserve a soaking after what you did to me. Go get him, Theo!'

The ensuing water fight ended up with them both soaked through but Ben didn't mind. As he carried Theo up the beach so Emily could change him into some dry clothes, he realised how lucky he was. The fact that he had a child of his own was a miracle. That Emily loved him was another one. If it weren't for the fact that he was needed at the clinic, he would have cancelled this trip. Every minute he was apart from Emily and Theo was a minute too long.

Saying goodbye to Emily the following day was the hardest thing Ben had had to do in ages. What made it worse was that he had no idea when he'd be able to return. He still needed to sort out the problems with the clinic's funding and that could take a while. He

drove straight to the clinic when he reached Paris, not
wanting to waste any time. His second in command,
Alexandrine Allain, was in her office so Ben was able
to catch up on what had happened in his absence. He
was relieved to learn that there had been few mishaps.
Once he sorted out the current problems, he thought,
he could leave Alexandrine in charge again.

By the time he made it home to his apartment, it was
almost midnight. He had intended to phone Emily but
he decided it was too late to call her then. He texted
her instead, just a brief message to tell her that he loved
and missed her. When his phone rang a moment later,
he smiled. Emily must have been waiting for his call,
proof of how much she was missing him too.

'And why aren't you asleep, *chérie*?' he demanded.

'Because I can't sleep. It's so lonely in this great big
bed without you.'

Ben felt heat scorch along his veins as he pictured
her lying in the bed they had shared the night before.
'I wish I was there with you,' he said huskily. 'You
wouldn't be lonely then.'

'I certainly wouldn't.' Her voice echoed with the
same memories and he sighed.

'I didn't realise how hard it was going to be, *chérie*.
We've only been apart for a few hours but it feels like
for ever.'

'It does. Let's hope you can get back here before
too long.'

'I don't know how long it will take to sort out the
problems with the funding,' he explained. 'It could take

several weeks and I can't leave while negotiations are taking place.'

'In that case, why don't Theo and I visit you? Don't worry—I understand that you'll have to work but at least we'd be able to spend some time together, plus it would be the ideal opportunity to show Theo around so that he has an idea where he'll be living when we move there.'

'What a wonderful idea!' Ben exclaimed.

'Isn't it?' She laughed. 'Theo will be thrilled when I tell him. He's not stopped talking about what a brilliant time he had at the beach yesterday. I think he sees you as his hero, Ben.'

'Does he?' Ben's heart swelled and he laughed. 'In that case, you've definitely got to bring him to see me.'

Emily promised that she would try to arrange some time off work the following week before they reluctantly hung up. Ben took a shower and got into bed but it was a long time before he fell asleep. What Emily had said about feeling lonely applied to him too, he thought wryly. Still, he only had to get through this week and he would see her again.

He fell asleep on that thought and his dreams were full of what the future held in store. They were going to have a wonderful life, him, Emily and Theo.

Emily waited until the Sunday morning to tell her parents what she and Ben had decided. Although every day on the farm was busy, Sundays tended to be slightly less so. She found her mother in the shop, stocking the refrigerator with a fresh batch of yoghurt.

'Darling, how lovely!' Frances exclaimed, closing the fridge door. She gave Emily a hug then picked up Theo and kissed him. 'And how's my favourite boy? Do you want a yoghurt, sweetheart?'

'Yes, please, Granny,' Theo said eagerly.

Frances took a pot of blueberry yoghurt out of the fridge and gave it to him. 'Why don't you sit behind the counter and eat it. You can tell me when any customers arrive and want to be served.'

Theo hurried off, pleased to be given such an important job. Frances turned to Emily and raised her brows. 'Am I right in thinking this isn't just a social call?'

Emily smiled ruefully. 'How did you guess?'

'Because you look both excited and nervous,' Frances told her bluntly. 'Has it something to do with Ben?'

'Yes.' Emily took a deep breath. It wasn't going to be easy to tell her mother that she and Theo were moving away. She knew how much Frances loved Theo and she was bound to be upset. 'I managed to convince him that it was wrong to cut himself off from Theo and me.'

'That's wonderful news!' Frances declared, hugging her. 'You two deserve to be happy after what you've been through. And as for Theo, well it can only be a good thing, in my view, to have his father around while he's growing up.'

'It will. He's really taken a shine to Ben,' Emily said eagerly. 'You should have seen the two of them when we were at the beach on Friday. It was Ben this and Ben that. Talk about hero worship!'

'Good. Having Theo accept Ben must be a huge weight off your mind,' Frances suggested.

Emily frowned. 'Funnily enough, it never occurred to me that Theo wouldn't accept him. It was the least of my worries, if I'm honest.'

'It's been hard for you, darling,' Frances said, patting her hand. 'I'm only glad that everything has worked out so well.'

'So am I, although I'm not sure how you'll feel about what else I have to tell you.'

'Go on,' Frances urged when she paused.

'Ben asked me if I'd consider moving to Paris and I said I would. He's needed at the clinic at the moment so it isn't feasible for him to stay in England.'

'I see.' Frances sighed. 'Obviously, I'll miss you and Theo but your place is with Ben, darling. I'd think if very strange if you two didn't want to live in the same country.'

'It won't be for ever,' Emily assured her. 'And you and Dad can come and visit any time you like.'

Frances laughed. 'That sounds like a wonderful idea. Not only will we get to see you and Theo, but I may finally persuade your father to take a holiday!'

They both laughed. Emily's heart was much lighter as they left the shop. Theo wanted to see the chickens so they made their way to the coop. A new batch of chicks had hatched that morning, much to Theo's delight. Emily smiled as she watched him scoop up one of the tiny bundles of fluff. Although Theo would miss all this when they moved to Paris, she was sure he would adapt. So long as he had her and Ben, he would be fine.

It was a busy week. As well as seeing patients, Ben attended several meetings with the clinic's bankers. His father had arranged the funding before he'd died and there was some concern about Ben's ability to run it the way Serge Legrange had outlined. Fortunately, he was able to allay their fears but it meant that his days started early and ended late. He spoke to Emily every day, needing to hear her voice even if he couldn't be with her. He couldn't wait for the weekend when he would see her and Theo again.

Friday turned out to be particularly hectic and Ben was kept busy all day. He felt completely drained when he got home and it didn't help that he seemed to have developed a cough which grew worse as the evening wore on. He went to bed as soon as he'd spoken to Emily and spent a restless night. It was a relief when it was time to get up. He drove to the airport, unable to contain his delight when he saw Emily and Theo walking through Customs. It may only have been a week since he'd seen them but it felt much longer!

'It's so good to see you both,' he declared. He kissed Emily then swung Theo up into his arms. 'Did you enjoy flying on the plane, *mon petit*?'

'Yes.' Theo's face lit up. 'It made this big noise— *whoosh*!'

Ben laughed. 'That *is* a big noise.' He put his arm round Emily and steered her towards the exit. 'I thought we could drop your bag at the apartment and then take a trip down the river.'

'That would be lovely but don't you have to work?' she said, smiling up at him.

'Not today.' He dropped a kiss on her nose. 'Today

I'm playing truant, and tomorrow too so I can spend some time with you. Promise you won't tell anyone.'

'Promise!' She laughed and Ben felt his heart kick into overdrive when he saw the delight on her face. If Theo hadn't been there, he would have kissed her until they were both breathless. He had to content himself with the thought that there would be plenty of time for that later.

Theo loved sailing down the River Seine on one of the bateaux mouches, the tourist boats which ferry people up and down the river. He also loved the trip up the Eiffel Tower, squealing with excitement as the lifts carried them higher and higher. They had an early dinner in the Tower's restaurant, another experience Theo enjoyed. Ben was delighted by his response and said so to Emily.

'I was worried in case Theo might be bored but he seems to have enjoyed himself.'

'He has.' Emily squeezed his hand. 'I have too. Thank you for a really lovely day, Ben.'

'It was my pleasure,' he said truthfully, his voice grating with emotion. His heart swelled as it struck him that there would be other wonderful days like this to come, days they would spend doing things together. As a family.

The thought stayed with him as he carried a sleepy Theo back to the apartment. Emily put him to bed in the spare room then came back to the sitting room where Ben was waiting. She smiled wistfully as she joined him by the window.

'Today has been so perfect, I don't want it to end.'

Ben drew her into his arms. 'There'll be other days just as perfect,' he said softly.

'You're right.' She rose on tiptoe and kissed him. 'We have a lifetime of perfect days to look forward to. And perfect nights, too.'

Ben's breath caught when he saw the invitation in her eyes. All of a sudden the passion that he'd kept in check came roaring to the surface. Sweeping her up into his arms, he carried her into his bedroom and laid her on the bed then lay down beside her.

'*Je t'aime*, Emily.'

'*Je t'aime*, Ben,' she whispered back.

They made love with a passion that overwhelmed them both. Whether it was the week-long absence that had stoked their hunger for each other, Ben wasn't sure. All he knew was that he wanted her so much that he felt he would die if he didn't make love to her.

As they lay in each other's arms later, Ben knew that he had never felt so complete. He had Emily's love, he had Theo, he had everything he could want. When that pesky cough started again, he tried to ignore it but it wouldn't go away. He was also drenched with sweat, he realised, and felt as though he was running a fever.

'Shall I fetch you a drink of water?' Emily offered, raising herself up on her elbow to look at him.

'No. You stay here. I'll get it.'

He ran his finger down her cheek in lieu of a kiss and got out of bed. Going into the kitchen, he poured himself a glass of water, trying to ignore the alarm bells that were ringing in his head: the last time he'd felt like this was shortly before he was diagnosed with lymphoma.

Emily was half asleep when he went back to bed. 'All right?' she murmured sleepily.

'Fine.' Ben lay down beside her, feeling his heart thumping not with passion this time but dread. Was it possible the cancer had returned? The cough, the tiredness, the fever and the sweats could be indications that something was wrong. Although he hadn't noticed any swellings in his lymph nodes, he couldn't take that as proof everything was fine. He needed to speak to his oncologist and find out if he was right to be concerned.

He closed his eyes, trying to contain the feeling of devastation that filled him. If the cancer *had* come back, it changed everything. There was no way that he was prepared to let Emily and Theo suffer. It would have been hard enough for them several years down the line but this was just the start of their life together and that would make it so much worse. He would have to end their relationship, although he didn't dare tell Emily the truth. She would insist that it didn't make a difference, that she wanted to be there for him no matter what.

Ben knew he couldn't trust himself not to weaken, so he would have to take a hard line. At the end of her stay, he would tell Emily that he'd realised he had made a mistake and didn't love her. His heart ached at the thought. She would be desperately hurt of course, but it was better that it happened now rather than later. If he did need treatment, and it didn't work, she would suffer even more. He had to be cruel to be kind.

CHAPTER FIFTEEN

EMILY was surprised by how distant Ben seemed the following morning. Although he'd told her that he was taking Sunday off, he left for work as soon as they had finished breakfast. Although he kissed her before he left, it was more a perfunctory gesture rather than a true expression of his feelings. She sensed that he was eager to get away from her and it worried her. Had she done something to upset him?

She chewed it over as she got Theo ready to go to the park. Everything had been perfect yesterday; they'd both agreed on that. It had been perfect last night too when they'd made love. Ben certainly hadn't been faking how much he'd wanted her! So what had happened to make him act so offhand with her?

By the time Ben returned that evening, she felt sick from worrying about it. It didn't help that he was just as aloof as he'd been at breakfast. Although he asked about her day, there was no real interest in his voice. He was merely going through the motions, being polite, and she hated it. He was better with Theo, smiling when the little boy excitedly told him about playing on the swings and eating an ice cream. However, when she added a comment, his face closed up and he became distant once more. Emily's nerves were at breaking point as she tucked Theo up in bed. Something was going on and she intended to find out what it was.

Ben was in the kitchen when she went back. He was making coffee in the old-fashioned pot he preferred. He barely glanced at her when she went in and Emily's taut nerves stretched that bit more.

'What's going on, Ben? Why are you acting so strangely?'

'I don't know what you mean.' He gave one of those Gallic shrugs. 'I've been out all day so I cannot see how you can accuse me of behaving oddly.'

'Yes, you have been out. After you told me that you intended to take the day off, too.' Emily refused to be deterred if that was what he hoped. 'What made you decide to go into work?'

'There was something urgent I needed to do. I'd forgotten about it.'

Quite frankly, Emily didn't believe him. She glared at him, determined to get to the bottom of the matter. 'I don't believe you. You wouldn't forget something that important.'

'Your faith in me is touching. However, I'm as forgetful as the next person, sadly.'

The sarcasm in his voice brought the colour to her face. It was all she could do to stand there when she wanted to turn tail and hide until the real Ben returned, the kind and loving Ben she adored.

'Why are you being so horrible?' she asked, her voice breaking. 'Does it give you a kick to upset me?'

'Of course not.' He turned towards the stove, either to hide his feelings or because he couldn't bear to look at her.

'Then tell me what's wrong,' she pleaded, wishing she knew which it was. She crossed the room and stood in front of him so that he was forced to look at her. 'Something's going on, Ben, and I want to know what it is.'

'You're imagining things.' He reached past her to lift the pot off the hob. Maybe he did it too quickly, Emily wasn't sure, but she gasped when she felt drops of scalding hot coffee spatter her bare arm.

'Are you all right?' He put the pot down and took hold of her arm, his eyes filled with concern when he saw the tiny red marks on her skin.

'I'm fine,' she said shortly, her eyes filling with tears. It wasn't the coffee that had hurt, but the fact that Ben could behave this way. Had she been wrong, didn't he love her? Was this his way of showing her that he no longer wanted her in his life?

A sob welled from her lips before she could stop it. Ben said something harsh as he snatched a towel off the rack and soaked it in cold water. 'Here.'

He wrapped her arm in the cold wet fabric and led her into the sitting room, sitting her down on the sofa with a solicitude that made her cry all the harder. How could he be so tender and caring one minute and so aloof the next?

'I'm sorry, *chérie*. It didn't mean to shower you with coffee,' he said, unwrapping the dressing so he could examine her arm. He frowned. 'I don't think there's any permanent damage.'

'It's fine as I said. I'm not crying about my arm, Ben. I'm upset because I can't bear it when you treat me so coldly. I thought you loved me but it doesn't feel as though you do at the moment.'

She couldn't go on as another sob overwhelmed her. Ben drew her to him and she could feel the tremor that passed through him as he held her tightly against him.

'I do love you, Emily. I love you with all of my heart and every scrap of my being. You're everything to me. *Everything.*'

Emily knew he was telling her the truth and felt more confused than ever. 'Then why have you been so distant with me today? What's going on, Ben. Tell me!'

He stood up abruptly and went to the window. Emily could sense his indecision and her fears multiplied tenfold. He had to explain, had to tell her what was happening and why he was trying to push her away after everything they'd been through…

Shock seared through her and she gasped. All of a sudden, she understood why. There was only one reason that Ben would behave this way. Just one.

'Ha-has the cancer come back?'

The question hung in the air and she saw him flinch. His eyes were hollow when he turned, as though all the light had gone out of him.

'I'm not sure but it may have done.' He ran his hand over his hair and she could tell that he was trying to get a grip on himself because he didn't want to scare her. That he should worry about her at such a moment simply proved how much he loved her.

'What symptoms have you had?' she asked, realising that she needed to be practical. If she allowed her emotions to get the better of her, she wouldn't be able to help him. 'I know you were coughing last night—could that be a sign it's come back?'

'Yes. I've also felt exhausted recently, far more tired than I should be even allowing for the long hours I've been working.'

'I see. Anything else?'

'Night sweats and fever,' he said succinctly. 'They were what drove me to seek advice before, the sweats and the fever, along with the lumps I found in my groin, of course.'

'Have you found any more lumps?' she demanded, her heart racing in fear because it sounded very ominous.

He shook his head. 'No.'

'That's a good sign, surely?'

'Possibly.' He smiled thinly. 'I spoke to my oncologist today. I have an appointment with her in the morning, although she won't be able to confirm or deny my suspicions until I've had some tests done.'

'What kind of tests?' Emily demanded anxiously.

'Blood and X-rays, probably a PET scan as well.'

'How long will it take before you get the results?' Emily wanted to know.

'A couple of weeks, maybe three.'

'That long!' she exclaimed and he sighed.

'It all takes time, *chérie.*'

'Then I'll have to phone Simon and explain that I need to take more time off work,' she said, finding it easier to stick to practicalities.

'There's no need to do that,' Ben protested.

'Of course there is.' She got up and went to him, putting her arms around him. 'There is no way that I'm letting you go through this on your own, my darling. I'll come with you tomorrow, of course. And once we have the dates for your X-rays and scan sorted out then we can decide if it would be better if I took Theo home to stay with my parents. He might get bored if he has to sit around in the hospital for too long.'

'You are amazing,' Ben declared. He buzzed her cheek with a kiss. 'You make it all sound so simple.'

'I know it isn't simple but it's the only way I can cope.' She looked into his eyes. 'We can get through this, Ben, no matter what happens.'

'You almost make me believe that,' he said roughly.

'You have to believe it.' She kissed him on the lips. 'What we have is too precious to lose. If the cancer has come back, we have to fight it. Together.'

'Are you sure? If it has come back, I'll need months of treatment. I can't bear to think of you having to watch me go through all that, especially when we have only just got back together.'

'And I can't bear to think of you having to suffer,' she said, her voice catching. 'But if it's the only way to get rid of the cancer then we'll manage, Ben. We have to. I love you and need you. Theo loves and needs you too. You have to be strong for our sakes.'

'I shall,' he promised and meant it with every fibre

of his being. No matter what it took, he was going to fight this and win.

Emily held out her hand. 'Come to bed, Ben. It won't affect the outcome of all those tests but it will help.'

Ben took her hand, feeling his confidence surging back. Even if he had to undergo more treatment, it would work; it really would! They made love in his bed and he wasn't ashamed when he cried afterwards, wasn't afraid to admit how much it meant to have Emily there, holding him. He needed her so much, needed her love and support, her strength as well as her beauty. Turning to face her, he told her that and watched the love light up her eyes.

'I need you too, Ben, just as much. You're everything to me and I can't imagine a life without you and don't want to try. No matter what happens, I'll always be here for you,' she whispered and he knew that she meant it, knew that Emily would always be at his side, loving and caring for him.

He fell asleep on that thought, feeling more at peace with himself than he'd felt in years. Maybe there would always be a degree of uncertainty about the future but so long as Emily was with him, he could handle it. No matter how long they had—and please heaven it was years!—their lives would be better, richer, more fulfilled by having each other at its heart.

EPILOGUE

WINTER arrived in Bride's Bay with a suddenness that caught everyone unawares. People shook their heads as they tried to remember the last time it had snowed. Emily smiled to herself as she stepped in front of the mirror. Her wedding dress may have been designed by one of Paris's leading couture houses but the white velvet cloak her mother had run up on her old sewing machine was going to be the star of the show!

'Oh, darling, you look lovely!' Frances came into the bedroom to check on her progress and stopped dead. Tears welled to her eyes and she hastily blotted them away with a tissue. 'I mustn't cry or my mascara will run, but you look gorgeous.'

'Do you think so?' Emily did a little twirl, watching the feather-light silk organza swirl around her ankles. She had chosen a simple style, a fitted bodice finished with tiny seed pearls and a full skirt. However the quality of the workmanship had turned the dress into a real fairytale gown. It had been a gift from her future mother-in-law and Emily had accepted it in the spirit it had been meant. Ruth Legrange was as thrilled about welcoming her and Theo into the family as Emily was to join it.

She turned away from the mirror and picked up her phone. 'I'll just text Ben to make sure he's ready.'

'Isn't it supposed to be bad luck to communicate with the bridegroom on the wedding day?' Frances said, only half joking.

Emily laughed. 'Don't be so old-fashioned, Mum. Anyway, there's no way that Ben and I are going to have bad luck today or any day! It's all positives from now on.'

'I'm so glad the tests were clear. It must have been so worrying for you,' Frances said. 'You've been very brave.'

'Ben's the brave one,' Emily said immediately.

Frances shook her head. 'No. You played your part, darling, as you'll continue to play it. It's what marriage is all about, being there for one another through the bad times as well as the good.'

'Stop it or you'll have me crying and I don't want to arrive at church looking like a panda!' Emily admonished, sniffing.

'Sorry.' Frances gave her a hug then headed to the door. 'I'd better go and see what the boys are up to. Theo looks adorable in his little pageboy outfit, but he was trying to persuade your father to take him to see the chickens!'

Frances' expression spoke volumes as she hurried out of the room, and Emily laughed. If she was honest, she didn't care if Theo got into a bit of a mess. It wouldn't spoil the day. Nothing would.

She smiled as she texted Ben to tell him that she was ready and that she loved him. Although she'd had to return to England, she had insisted on being with him when he'd received the results of the tests. Neither of them had slept the night before and the tension had been unbearable as they had waited to be called into the oncologist's office. When the consultant had smilingly informed them that all the tests were clear and that the cancer hadn't returned, they'd been too elated to speak. It was the consultant's view that a viral infection had been to blame for Ben's symptoms, nothing more sinister. They had left the doctor's office and stood in the street and hugged one another. Then Ben had gone down on one knee and asked her to marry him and Emily hadn't hesitated. The future was all theirs and nothing was going stop them being together.

Emily's phone rang a few seconds later and she laughed when she saw Ben's name on the display. He didn't believe in bad luck any more than she did. 'Hello. How are you today?'

'Excited.'

Emily felt all her love for him well up inside her. Ben meant the world to her. He was her heart, her soul, her lover and her friend. 'Me too. Excited and so happy I could burst! In an hour's time I'm going to be your wife—what could be better than that?'

'Nothing,' Ben replied, his voice reflecting everything she was feeling. 'Absolutely nothing at all, *chérie*.'

* * * * *

MILLS & BOON®
Book Club
2 Free Books!

Get your free books now at

www.millsandboon.co.uk/freebookoffer

Or fill in the form below and post it back to us

THE MILLS & BOON® BOOK CLUB™—HERE'S HOW IT WORKS: Accepting your free books places you under no obligation to buy anything. You may keep the books and return the despatch note marked 'Cancel'. If we do not hear from you, about a month later we'll send you 5 brand-new stories from the Medical™ series, including two 2-in-1 books priced at £5.49 each and a single book priced at £3.49*. There is no extra charge for post and packaging. You may cancel at any time, otherwise we will send you 5 stories a month which you may purchase or return to us—the choice is yours. *Terms and prices subject to change without notice. Offer valid in UK only. Applicants must be 18 or over. Offer expires 31st July 2013. **For full terms and conditions, please go to www.millsandboon.co.uk/freebookoffer**

Mrs/Miss/Ms/Mr (please circle)
_____

First Name
_____

Surname
_____

Address
_____

_____
                                    Postcode
_____

E-mail
_____

Send this completed page to: Mills & Boon Book Club, Free Book Offer, FREEPOST NAT 10298, Richmond, Surrey, TW9 1BR

Find out more at
www.millsandboon.co.uk/freebookoffer

Visit us Online

0712/M2YEA